50 REAL GHOST STORIES OF FIRST RESPONDERS
HAUNTING TRUE STORIES OF GHOSTS ON THE JOB

EVE S EVANS

ALSO BY

EVE S EVANS

Fiction:

The Haunting of Hartley House

Hartley House Homecoming

The Haunting of Crow House

The Haunting of Redburn Manor

Origins

Anthologies:

True Ghost Stories of First Responders

50 Terrifying Ghost Stories

Holiday Hauntings

Shadow People

Chilling Ghost Stories

Haunted Hotels

Haunted Hospitals

Haunted Objects

Haunted People

For Kaitlin

Follow Eve and her books on Goodreads or Bookbub! And get notified of any new reads coming in 2022-2023.

The following stories are based on true events.

All rights reserved. No part of this publication may be transmitted or reproduced in any form or by any means. This includes photocopying, electronic, mechanical, or by storage system (informational or otherwise), unless given written permission by the author.

Copyright © May 2022 Eve S. Evans

1 WHERE THERE IS SMOKE

Like most people I became a firefighter because I wanted to help people. Growing up, I was always bigger and stronger than most of the other kids my own age. My parents had taught me that I should always fight and protect those who couldn't fight for themselves, so the job seemed like a natural fit. I dreamed of being the guy who would be there for someone when they needed me the most.

During my first few months in the department my superiors had to temper my enthusiasm and willingness to put myself in danger because it inevitably risked the lives of my colleagues when they'd have to go in and pull me out of a blaze. This story happened during one such night, and it is something, even fifteen years later, I carry with me.

Fifteen minutes. That is how long it had been since the call had come into the station. We had responded quickly, but I could feel every second like a blow to my chest. The truck roared underneath us as it sped through the streets, yet the watch on my wrist felt like it had begun running at twice its normal speed. Every tick meant the injuries were getting worse, more time meant death.

I hung my head and tapped my foot against the metal floor, anxious for our arrival. The helmet I would put on the moment I exited the truck hung loosely in my hands. I stared at the crest emblazoned on the front, a constant reminder of the virtues of a firefighter. Duty. Honor. Bravery. I didn't need to see them to know what they meant to me, what they meant to the men and women who wore this uniform.

I could smell the smoke even before I could see the fire. My eyes lifted from the helmet and I could see the black column of smoke rising to the heavens. My hands tightened reflexively and I could feel the hard plastic dig into my fingers. Black meant a man-made structure. The color was created from the plastics and rubbers that were in the walls of a building.

The engine revved a few hundred RPMs higher as our driver was urged forward by the smell. Thirty seconds later and I hear the squeal of the brakes and feel my body press forward against the seatbelt as the big truck comes to a stop. My body moves without my mind having to tell it to. The motion out has been practiced and performed hundreds of times so when the moment arrives it comes as easy as breathing.

My feet hit hard concrete and my knees bend slightly to cushion the impact. My partner hands me a mask before I slip my arms through the straps of the oxygen tank he is holding and he twists the knob at the top. I hear the air running through the tube and I secure the mask over my face and give him a thumbs up to let him know I can breathe. I turn to my right and grab the handle to one of the many compartments on the side of the truck. I already know what's inside, I put the pry bar in there myself after the last time I used it. My hand closes around the metal shaft.

I really looked at the building for the first time. It was a two story apartment building, with the doors to the units on the inside. I started to move toward the front door as my radio buzzed in my ears followed by my chief telling us to wait to make our entrance so the hose crew had a chance to get some water on the flames. My adrenaline was spiking and I bounced from foot to foot as I waited for the go ahead.

I could feel the heat radiating off the structure as I watched two powerful jets of water flash into view from behind me. The drenched the front entrance and begun moving upwards to the second floor where most of the smoke seemed to be coming from. My radio came to life again and my chief told me and my partner to enter the building, but to be careful and stay in contact. We acknowledged his orders and made our way through the front door.

The main lobby looked much as it probably had most days. The fire hadn't yet spread to this part of the building, but that didn't mean we were safe. The roof would weakened as the fire ate its way through the floors upstairs and could lead to the entire building collapsing on top of us without even seeing the fire. This knowledge had us moving from door to door quickly, banging on each one announcing that we were from the fire department. When no one answered, we moved on to the next door. If the fire had spread to this part of the building we would have used the pry bars to wedge open the door to ensure everyone had gotten out of the building.

The check of the first floor went very quickly. Either everyone had gotten out or they hadn't been home when the fire had started. We radioed this in to the guys outside and they told us to move up to the second floor but to be careful, they had yet to fully contain the blaze. Just then the two of us heard several loud thumps coming from up above us. They were too constant in sound and pace to be something falling. To me it sounded like someone running.

"Did you hear that?" I asked my partner.

He nodded in response. "Sounded like footsteps. Someone's up there."

We were already in a race against time, and now things just got more serious. We radioed in that it sounded like someone was upstairs and we were going to try and get them out. We'd seen the elevator in the hallway and had to assume that the stairwell was somewhere nearby.

It didn't take long to locate the stairs. The door was right next to the elevator. The sound of our boots pounding up the stairs seemed to echo in the small space as we raced up to the second floor. When we arrived at the door I pulled off my glove and touched the handle. It was warm, but not hot. It meant the fire could be nearby but it hadn't yet reached the other side of the door. I turned the handle and we were enveloped by a wave of smoke.

One moment I had been looking at a door and the next I couldn't see anything. I waved my hand a little bit, more out of instinct than any real intention of it accomplishing anything. I got down on my hands and knees and saw that I could at least see a little ways through the smoke. The thickest parts were still above us and we could at least see our surroundings as we tried to locate the person we'd heard up here.

"Hello! Fire Department! We're here to help you out of the building!" I yelled.

There was no response, but the mask does muffle your voice a great deal so I continued to move my way deeper into the building. The smoke didn't seem to be getting any thicker so I hoped that meant the water was doing the trick of putting out the fire. I reached a door and banged on it. It swung open and slammed against the wall. I assumed that whoever lived here hadn't shut it in their haste to escape the fire. Still I called out into the unit and didn't hear any response. I couldn't leave the area unchecked though and I crawled my way in.

The air was fairly clear, allowing me to stand up and move about more freely. I shut the door, hoping to block the smoke long enough for me to make my way through the entire apartment. It was clear from the get go that this particular apartment was vacant. There was no furniture anywhere which made clearing the room extremely fast.

I made my way back to the front door and prepared to leave. When I went to turn the handle I heard what sounded like someone running down the hall. I swung the door open, hoping my partner hadn't run into some sort of trouble. The smoke rushed in, but I managed to catch a what appeared to be the silhouette of a person as they ran through the smoke.

The first thing I knew for certain it wasn't my partner that I'd seen. The size was all wrong. The person I'd seen was at least a half a foot shorter and they hadn't been wearing a helmet like he'd been when I last seen him. The other thing was, I'd have heard the hissing of the oxygen tank he was wearing if it had been him.

So, I'd found the source of the footsteps, but if they continued to run around in the smoke, they were sure to collapse. It seemed a miracle that it hadn't happened already. I radioed my partner and told him that I'd seen a person running through the halls and I needed his help locating them.

His response was immediate. "Running through the halls?" From the sound of his voice, he seemed just as surprised as I was.

I got back down on all fours and began crawling in the direction I'd seen the person running. I heard a door click closed behind me and knew that my partner was close behind. We moved as quickly and safely as we could looking in both directions. The elevator came into view and then the stairwell, but both of them were closed and I'd assumed that we'd have heard it if someone had used either.

We kept moving forward, but there was no other doors and most importantly there nobody was in the hall. This would have been the time where I'd have stood up and looked around confused but that wasn't an option at this point.

"Hello? Is someone there?" Other than the sound of my oxygen, there wasn't a response. I turned around and looked at my partner. "Anything?" He shook his head. I was perplexed. There was only one other thing I could check. I radioed the chief to ask if anyone had come out of the building and he told me that no one had left. His tone left no doubt to the validity of the answer.

I looked back again and my partner gave me a shrug. What else was he supposed to do. At this point we returned the way we had come and checked the last of the rooms. We didn't find anyone there either.

On our way back I kept replaying what I'd seen when I opened the door. I considered that it had just been the smoke making me see things, but I know I'd seen a person running by as I opened the door. I'd heard them just outside the thin piece of wood. It just didn't make sense for someone to disappear like that, but that's just what had happened.

We made our way back to the stairs and outside of the building. At this point the hose crews had all but doused what remained of the fire and were clearing the few hotspots that remained. When the two of us took our masks off I could see the questioning look I was getting from my partner, I didn't blame him. It didn't make sense to me either, but I wasn't in the mood to hear it. If we'd missed someone up there and it had cost a life I was going to be crushed.

That didn't end up being the case though. Another truck had arrived and they took the job of searching the building a second time while we cooled off for a bit. They were done with the search quickly and told us that there wasn't anyone in the building. The greater part of me was relieved to hear that, but it still left me with lingering questions that didn't have any clear answers.

Even years later, I swear to seeing a person running down that hall. There isn't anything I can do to prove what I'd seen was really there. There are plenty of stories you hear from long time vets about seeing and hearing things that don't make sense. This just happens to be my story. Make of it what you will.

2 EMPTY

It was some time after midnight, and I was doing my usual patrol around town. It was fairly quiet on the roads, since it was the middle of the week, and the streets were empty too. I figured it was going to be an uneventful night, and continued to cruise along at a reasonable speed, making sure to check alleyways as I passed them in case there was anything going on in the shadows.

Ahead of me was a bridge that crossed over the town's river. This area wasn't very well lit, even more so when there were no other cars around, so I slowed down.

Just as I started to cross the bridge, something caught the corner of my eye. It was a woman, standing by the side of the road a short distance ahead of me. The bridge had railings, but they weren't very visible in the darkness, and the area had a history of people committing suicide by jumping into the river below.

I only glimpsed her face briefly in my headlights, but something about her expression seemed distressed, and I feared she might be hurt, or planning on jumping. There were no other cars around, so I immediately pulled over to the side of the road to check on her.

I left the engine running so that the headlights would continue illuminating the area, and climbed out of the patrol car, getting my badge ready.

But the moment I stepped out, my heart sank in dread. The street was empty. The woman was nowhere to be seen.

Had she already jumped? There'd been barely a few seconds between seeing her standing there to getting out of the car. Maybe seeing me pull up had caused her to panic and go over the edge.

Fearing the worst, I hurried over to where she'd been standing, and peered over the side of the bridge.

It was too dark to see anything at first, but as my eyes adjusted, I saw something. There was a large dark shape protruding from the water below, and it took me a moment to realize what I was seeing; a car, half-submerged in the river.

I hastily overcame my shock and grabbed my radio, calling for immediate back-up. I didn't know how long the car had been in the water, but if there was any chance of saving those inside, I had to take it.

After confirming the location through the radio, and double checking the woman wasn't still standing by the road, I jumped back into my car and turned on my lights and siren. It wasn't necessary since there were no cars, but it was an added precaution while I hit the gas pedal and sped across the bridge, heading down to the riverside.

By the time I arrived, another patrol car was there, and the diving crew were en route. It wasn't safe going into the water without proper equipment and strategy. All I could do was hope that the car hadn't been in the water long, and there was still a chance to rescue those inside.

During this time, though, I couldn't help but wonder who that woman was, or where she had gone. There was nobody else in the water that I could see; just the car, with only its back trunk sticking out. I hadn't seen her fall or heard her hit the water either, so it was unlikely she'd jumped, but it was impossible for her to have simple disappeared like that.

Luckily, the diving crew and ambulance arrived shortly after, and they were able to immediately get into the water. The paramedics and I waited anxiously on the riverbank for the survivors, but I already had a sinking feeling in my stomach that we were too late.

The diving crew managed to pull two bodies from the car and bring them to shore. One was a woman, the other was a young boy – presumably her son – who had been sitting in the backseat. Neither were breathing.

The paramedics immediately got to work trying to resuscitate them on the scene. It was a tense few minutes, watching them work.

Eventually, they managed to revive the young boy, and he was transported immediately to the hospital.

The woman never made it. The paramedics tried for twenty minutes to bring her back, but she never drew breath. Only the boy survived the accident.

It was only afterwards, once the panic and chaos of the incident had calmed down, that I realized where the woman on the side of the road had gone. She'd been inside the car. She was the woman they'd been unable to revive.

I remember the utter shock and horror of that realization. The woman I'd seen on the side of the road had been the same woman trapped inside the sinking car. She must have already been dead, and the figure I'd seen was her spirit, trying to warn me about the accident below, desperate for me to save her son.

That whole night had a huge impact on me and the way I saw things after that. It was one of the creepiest, most harrowing nights of my life, and it's one that I'll never forget.

3 A SHOT IN THE DARK

A few years ago something strange happened while I was on patrol. I had been called to respond on a number of small incidents. These were things that you'd see every night on the job trespassers, domestic disputes, loitering that kind of thing. I figured it was going to be a normal night when a call went out to all officers in the vicinity of a certain residential area that everything changed.

The dispatcher had described someone screaming and the sound of gunshots being heard by one of the people who lived there. The area in question was an empty parking lot that had a reputation as a place where kids liked to hang out, do a little underage drinking and possibly some drugs. Most nights when I would drive by it wasn't uncommon to see people scatter at the sight of my car turning the corner. There were a number of occasions where there'd been some minor scraps, but a shooting wasn't something I would have expected.

Even though my job carries with it a level of danger that most jobs do not, I had yot at this point had to discharge my weapon in the line of duty. Sure, I'd had to point it at a few suspects, but shooting someone is something that no officer wants to experience. So when the call of "shots fired" came, my heart rate kicked up a little bit. Still, this was my job and I hoped that I could deescalate the situation without using my weapon. I grabbed the radio and informed dispatch I in route to the scene, put my car in gear and headed off in that direction.

In most cases I would use my lights and siren to cover the four blocks quickly, but with a gun involved, they can actually make people nervous. Even so, traffic that evening was light allowing me to covered the distance to the vacant lot quickly.

At night you could always tell when you were coming close to this particular place. The area was fairly large and vandals had taken it upon themselves to break out all of the lights the city had installed. This made the entire area almost completely pitch black, which normally wouldn't have meant much, but this call wasn't your ordinary one.

I radioed to dispatch that I'd arrived on the scene before reaching over and turning on the spotlight. I started scanning the area for any signs that someone was still there, but the area I could see was limited at best. In the daytime the lot is fairly large, initially designed to hold almost 200 cars at one time, but when the only area I could see came from the small beam the light was producing made it seem that much bigger.

I reached for the handle, figuring it would be easier to get out and take a look, but I stopped myself. If someone had a gun, then I'd just let them know I was there. I heard two other officers respond to the call on the way here and it would be better if all of us went in together.

Another five minutes passed before the other two officers arrived and the three of us could coordinate how we were going to enter the area. It was decided that we would turn on all of our spotlights and shine them in the same direction then move in with our backs to the lamps. This way if someone did fire on us it seemed that the bright bulbs might obstruct their vision.

We all moved in a straight line, but kept enough distance between each other so we didn't make ourselves easy targets. I braced my flashlight in one hand under my service weapon as we entered the lot. At the time it felt like every muscle in my body was a coiled spring, ready to react at the first sign of danger. I was sure my heart was going to explode out of my chest it was beating so hard. Even so, I knew I had to keep my mind on the task at hand. Any distraction, any slip could mean I could get shot, or worse, one of the other officers who were trusting me to have their backs.

We moved in a grid pattern, ensuring we covered every single part of the lot before we returned to our vehicles. None of us really thought that we'd find someone there with a gun, <u>it would be foolish to stick around after discharging it in public</u> to stick around. Really we were there to ensure that if someone had been hurt we could call in the paramedics.

[margin note: grammar]

Now that I could relax and the adrenaline in my blood had started to dissipate I felt exhausted. I could have sworn I'd worked a double shift and yet I still had another six hours before I could go home. Mostly though I was relieved that nothing had happened. I wished the other officers a good night and went to reach for the handle when the unmistakeable crack of a gun shattered the night air, followed by a man wailing in pain.

Immediately all of us jumped behind the nearest cruiser, which just happened to be mine at the time. My training had taken over and I had instinctively drew my weapon and had it pointed in the direction of the abandoned lot. It seemed impossible what had just happened. We'd canvassed the entire area and come up with nothing, no people, no victims, not even a spent shell casing.

Even in my hyper aware state I found myself going over the search of the area, trying to pick out a place where we could have missed someone. I know that I'd look carefully, but no one was perfect and in the dark, it was possible we'd passed right next to someone unaware that they'd been there. The one positive thing about the gunshot is we knew the general direction from which it had come from.

All three of us took turns yelling out to the assailant to abandon their weapon and come towards the light with their hands up. Not only did the person not follow instructions, none of us could illicit a response. The longer we waited the more it seemed we were going to have to go after them. A prospect none of us were happy about. From the scream we'd heard, it was obvious they were willing to use the weapon, which ratcheted up the danger considerably.

We aimed our spotlights in the direction of the noise, only to see that our view was blocked by a wall that hid an area where a dumpster will once sat. Because of this, even the bright lights mounted to the cars, we couldn't see anything. The sound had clearly been from that part of the lot and it appeared like we'd have to investigate on foot. Moving would mean abandoning our cover but with a person hurt and possibly dying, we knew we couldn't wait any longer.

All of us moved at once, moving at a dead run, hoping to take the suspect by surprise. The beam of my light bounced up and down as I rushed across the empty space in front of me, gun at the ready. We ate up the distance quickly, and I could see more and more of the walled off area.

I was ten feet away and I found an extra gear as I rushed into the open, ready to fire the instant I saw a gun pointed at me. I pointed the flashlight in the dark space, I could feel my finger pulling against the trigger and it depress just slightly, a feather away from discharging. My eyes found the corners, seeking, only there was a problem... nobody was there.

I turned in a half circle, still ready, but it also was empty. Slowly I lowered my weapon, and stood up straight. Something wasn't right here, and I wasn't sure what it was. I shivered slightly as a chill went down my spine. I almost expected someone to pop out at any moment, taking all of us by surprise, but that didn't happen.

We made another sweep of the area, and then moved to the rest of the lot, this time taking almost twice the time the first search did. Again, we found no person, no spent casings, in fact there was no evidence that anyone had been there at all. We even checked for traces of blood in case the person who we all had heard scream had gotten away, and again we came up with nothing.

In all we probably spent about an hour at that parking lot, only to feel equally freaked out and stupid at the same time. I know for a fact that someone hadn't run out of there after we'd heard the shot and the scream. One of us would have seen or heard them, I'm sure of that. I like to think of myself as a rational person but I couldn't say what happened.

The truth is, I'm not sure what happened at there that night. I'm glad that there had been two other officers who'd experienced the same thing otherwise I'm not sure anyone would have believed the story. I know I wouldn't have. You hear a lot of weird things when it comes to places people have died, but you always think of them as fishing stories, things that have been exaggerated and changed over time. This is my story... believe what you will.

4 AMISS

I was sitting in my patrol car, taking a brief lunch break. I had parked across the street from a grocery store, since I'd happened to be in the area and there were plenty of spaces.

While I was flicking through a newspaper, eating my lunch, something caught my attention. Ahead of me, standing outside the grocery store, was a woman. She was frantically waving her arms at me, a panicked look on her face, as though she was trying to get my attention. There was something slightly *off* about her, though I couldn't quite put my finger on it at the time. I remember thinking that she looked unusually pale, to the extent that she was almost translucent, but I figured it must have been a reflection of the light or something making it seem like that.

Thinking she might be in some kind of distress, I quickly put down the paper and drove the car over to the grocery store.

In those brief few minutes of pulling into the parking lot and heading towards the store, the woman had disappeared. I looked around the area, but I couldn't see her anywhere, and no cars had driven off during this time.

Assuming she must have gone inside the grocery store, I climbed out of my car and headed inside. I didn't know what to expect. It might have been nothing after all, but as an officer, it was obviously my duty to make sure everything was okay.

The moment I stepped inside, I immediately noticed something was off. Everyone looked terrified, some crouching behind the shelves and trying to hide. Nobody even looked my way as I entered; they were all focused on something elsewhere in the store, which I couldn't see. Judging by people's reactions, I knew something was wrong.

    I drew my weapon and called for backup as quietly as I could, so as not to alarm anyone who might have been armed and dangerous.

    Moving as swiftly as I could, I crouched behind one of the shelves and peered round.

    A man was standing in the middle of the aisle, waving a gun around. Two people were lying on the ground at his feet, and I could see a lot of blood around the bodies. A little way behind him was another body, lying half-in and half-out of the aisle. None of them were moving.

    I'd warned backup to keep their sirens off and enter quietly, but in the meantime, I had to do what I could to apprehend the suspect before there were any more fatalities.

Waiting for him to turn his back to me, I moved from my hiding spot and managed to disarm him, pulling his gun out of his hand and warning him not to move.

Backup arrived shortly afterwards, and once the suspect had been taken away, we began to assess the fatalities.

There were three dead, and another critically injured. One of the witnesses explained the situation to us; the man had stormed into the store, waving his gun around and shouting something about how his girlfriend had cheated on him with another man. We later found out that his girlfriend worked at that grocery store, and that she was one of the victims. She had been shot first, and the injuries were too severe; there was no hope of saving her or the other two victims. Since the man had a silencer on his gun, nobody outside the store had any idea what was going on.

As soon as I saw the girlfriend's face, I felt a strange sense of dread overcome me. It was the woman I'd seen outside of the grocery store; the one who had been waving frantically at me in distress.

But if she'd been shot first, then how had she managed to flag me down like that? It was impossible that the woman I'd seen outside was the same woman who was lying dead in the grocery store, but I knew I hadn't made a mistake.

To this day I don't really know what I saw, but I knew my eyes weren't deceiving me. The two women were the same.

Perhaps it was the spirit of the man's girlfriend, warning me about the situation occurring inside. Or maybe it was something else that I didn't understand. Either way, if it hadn't been for her warning, there may have been more fatalities that day.

5 FLAT-LINER

I was working as a paramedic when we got a call that someone had OD'd. We raced to the scene as fast as we could, knowing that time was of the essence in situations like this.

When we arrived, the man was already flat-lining. We immediately loaded him into the back of the ambulance and continued to work on reviving him for the whole drive to the hospital. It's always a tense and exhausting ordeal trying to bring someone back from the brink of death, especially knowing that the more time that passes, the less likely it is that we'll succeed.

I was starting to get tired after constant compressions, so my partner took over from me. Just as I stepped back from the patient, I felt something touch my hand, and a voice whispered in my ear: "It's okay. Let me go."

My partner was nowhere near me at the time, and my hand wasn't touching anything either, but I could have sworn I felt someone touch it.

Of course we didn't let him go. We kept trying to revive him all the way to the hospital, taking it in turns to give him CPR until we got tired.

He arrived at the hospital DOA. There was nothing else we could do for him. It's always hard, knowing when to let go, knowing when someone's a lost cause. But as a paramedic, you have to make that call and know when a person is beyond saving.

Even after we got him to the hospital and went on to the next call, I couldn't get my mind off that voice I'd heard, or the feeling of someone touching my hand. I have to wonder if it was all in my imagination, just my mind playing tricks on me while I was battling exhaustion and desperation. Or if it really was a sign from beyond; the man telling us to let him go, that he was already passing on and it was too late to bring him back.

Maybe it was my own guilt tripping me up. Despite my many years as a paramedic, it never gets easier when you're unable to help someone. It really makes you question if you could have done more.

In this case, the man was too far gone by the time we reached him. And after trying to revive him for over half an hour, there was nothing else we could have done.

6 UNRESPONSIVE

Summer is one of the hardest and most stressful times for a first responder. Especially when you're dealing with kids. There are so many accidents this time of year, especially around water, and not all of them have a happy ending.

This summer, we were called to a residence where a child had drowned in a swimming pool. Just getting a call like that, you immediately fear the worst.

My crew and I headed to the address as soon as we could. When we arrived, the family was performing CPR on a young girl. She was laying on the ground beside the pool, unresponsive. We later found out that she was only six years old. They'd been trying to resuscitate her since they'd called for the ambulance, but so far they'd had no luck and received no response. My partner and I swiftly took over, hopeful that we could bring her back since it hadn't been too long ago that she'd been pulled from the water.

The child's mother was in hysterics, and the rest of her family were heartbroken as we did all that we could to bring her back.

While my partner was performing CPR on her, I was monitoring her blood pressure, waiting for a response. But it was clear after a few minutes that we were too late. Nevertheless, none of us were willing to give up on her, and we kept working on her, trying desperately to bring her back.

All of a sudden, the air around me turned cold, even though the sun was still shining, and I broke out completely in goosebumps.

That's when I heard it. A child's giggle, from somewhere behind me.

It sounded so out of place against the family's sobs that I gasped, turning my head to look behind me. A little girl was walking along the hedges behind me, smiling and laughing to herself. As soon as she went behind the bushes, she seemed to disappear, her laughter trailing off into silence, and the strange coldness I'd felt before vanished too.

When I turned back to look at the child on the ground in front of us, I was overcome with complete shock. It was the same girl I'd just seen walking behind me. Completely identical.

My partner was getting tired at this point and asked me to take over, so I tried to get what I'd seen out of my mind as I worked on trying to revive the child.

We kept working on her for a while, but it was obvious she wasn't coming back to us. The whole ordeal really shook me up. Being unable to help a child who had drowned was one thing, but I couldn't get the fact that I'd seen her spirit too – or at least, that's what I thought I saw. There were no other children in the area, and the girl didn't have any siblings. I was certain that the girl I'd seen looked exactly like the child we'd been trying to revive.

I thought about the incident a lot afterwards, constantly questioning what I'd seen.

I liked to think it was the girl's spirit departing, because she'd seemed happy. Her laughter was the last thing I'd heard from her. And that meant she wasn't held back by any kind of sorrow or regret.

I'd always been a sceptic when it came to things like the paranormal. I'd never believed in ghosts or the afterlife. But after that day, everything changed. It made me wonder if there really was something more after death.

I hope that the little girl managed to find peace, even if her family couldn't.

7 HOLD ON

Flames leapt from the roof of the two-story office building as we pulled up in the engine. Most of the fire was concentrated on both floors on the right but was likely to spread quickly. Sweat was already trickling down my forehead and stinging my eyes. Even from where I stood, the intensity of the heat was oppressive. Anyone still inside wouldn't last long. We had to hurry.

We were the third truck on the scene; hoses were already deployed and were saturating the structure with jets of water. I quickly donned my mask and oxygen tank and prepared to enter the building to find anyone who might have been trapped inside. With me was Henry. He was a thirteen-year veteran firefighter and one of my best friends. From the beginning, he had taken me under his wing. After eight years of working together, we trusted each other implicitly.

We gave each other's equipment a quick check and ran towards the door to the building. The other crews had concentrated their efforts on the front door, knowing we would be going in, so most of the major flames had been extinguished in this area, giving a relatively safe point of entry. Henry went in first, and I was right on his tail. It was time to go to work.

We worked side by side; a method honed from years of experience with one another. Knowing anyone who would have been in the offices to the left would have been able to evacuate without much trouble, so we learned to focus our efforts on the part of the building where the fire originated from. All of this was communicated to one another without a spoken word.

The hallways to the building were set up in a giant ring, with two halls running through the center. I indicated I would take the hall to the right while Henry would take the rightmost passage in front of us. Fire axe in hand, I went door to door checking for people, but all the rooms were either unoccupied or empty.

My thoughts were interrupted by the radio crackling to life. "Hey Tom, I found someone, but I'm going to need your help."

"Gotcha, I'm on my way."

I turned around and made my way back down the corridor. The further I went, the heat from the flames only increased. In the back of my mind, I knew this part of the building was already dangerous as the flames ate through the support beams, and the building would collapse on top of us. Almost on cue to my left, I heard a crashing noise as something gave way.

I stopped as a chill forced its way through me. "Henry! Are you okay?" No response came. It wasn't like Henry not to respond. Worry drove me faster down the hall as I rushed to make sure he was okay. Again and again, I tried him on the radio, but his voice never came through.

Turning the corner, I looked down the hall at my worst fears. Pieces of the ceiling had collapsed and were partially blocking the way forward. I hoped that Henry was okay but, in my gut, I knew something was wrong.

I had to pick my way through the debris that was strewn all over the floor. Every part of me wanted to rush forward and brave the flames, but if I were injured too, then neither one of us would be leaving. So, I forced myself to go slow and take my time. Each second felt like an eternity as I checked each room for signs of Henry.

The fifth door I looked into was a wall of flames, and I almost skipped it, but I caught something out of the corner of my eye. A body lay slumped over, and I saw a firefighter kneeling next to it. Relief washed through me, but I still had to find a way in. I could cut my way through the wall, but it would take too long. That left one choice. I stepped back and made a running leap, cutting through the fire.

Landing on my feet, I quickly surveyed the scene in front of me. A woman lay crumpled against the wall, but Henry wasn't next to her any longer. I turned to see if he had moved deeper into the office. What I saw didn't make sense. A large beam had crashed through the ceiling, and beneath it was a person wearing a firefighter uniform. I had thought Henry and I were the only ones on this side of the building. How was this other person here?

The surprise shifted to panic when I saw the familiar markings of the suit. It was Henry. There wasn't any doubt in my mind. The beam on top of him had to weigh nearly 800 lbs., far too large for me to lift on my own.

"Henry! Talk to me! Say something to let me know you're still with me." When he didn't move or speak, I quickly radioed in that there was a firefighter down, and we needed help.

In the meantime, I went over to check on the woman. Her face was covered in soot, but I could see the slight rise and fall of her breathing. At least she was still alive.

"Are you okay?" I asked her.

Her eyes fluttered open, and a series of coughs racked her entire body. She had taken in a lot of smoke and needed medical help, and *soon*. I had two people in trouble, and until help arrived, there was only one of me.

The next few minutes I spent going back and forth between the two of them. Making sure the woman was breathing and trying to tamp out any of the flames that had spread on the beam as he lay there pinned.

When the team of firefighters arrived, they put out the fire near the door with a portable extinguisher and entered the room. One person lifted the woman off the floor and disappeared through the door. The rest of us went over and carefully lifted the beam, freeing Henry.

Even with the obstruction removed, he still didn't show any sign of consciousness. Left with no other choice, I hoisted him over my shoulder and carried him outside. Laying him on the ground, I pulled off his mask and checked for a pulse. The familiar beat was absent, and we began CPR. We continued to do so for nearly ten minutes before accepting that he was gone. It still didn't make sense though, I know I had seen him helping the woman just moments before. How was that possible when he had been trapped?

Henry's death hit me hard. I'd known other firefighters that had died in the line of duty, but never anybody I was close with. He was like a big brother to me, and now he was just gone.

To try and move on, I wanted to meet the woman he saved when giving up his own life. I wanted to ask her if she knew what had happened. That, and if she had seen the firefighter next to her just before I arrived. I wanted answers to the questions that wouldn't give me peace.

Oxygen was being fed into her nose along with an IV tube running into one of her arms when I arrived. A confused look passed over her face when I entered her room, but when she looked at the crest on my shirt denoting that I was a firefighter, she smiled.

I tried to return the smile, but it didn't reach my eyes. "Nice to see you are recovering."

"Yeah, the doctor says I can go home in a day or two. Are you the one who saved me?"

"No, that would have been Henry. I just found you both and called for help."

She looked back and forth as if expecting to see someone else there. "Is he here too?"

The fake smile that I had plastered on my face fell. "Unfortunately, he didn't make it. The beam that fell on him caused a number of internal injuries."

I expected to see a look of sadness come over her, but that was the opposite of what happened. Her eyes widened in shock. "That beam was about to crush me, and he pushed me out of the way. But I thought he was fine because he was there the entire time telling me to hold on, that help was coming."

The look on my face must have matched hers because she told me that no one else had believed her either. That she had just mistaken me for Henry, but she was insistent that hadn't been the case. Nobody had believed her story, though.

I was here for answers, and that meant telling her what I had seen myself, how I had seen someone kneeling next to her right before I jumped into the office, and that he was gone just moments later. If just one of us had seen something, it would be easier to dismiss, but both of us? Not as likely.

What happened in that room that day? Was it Henry's spirit comforting the woman in a time of crisis? I don't know. There are other stories that would suggest this, where the spirits of firefighters show up to give comfort in a time of crisis. I wouldn't put this past him; he lived for that job and always talked about wanting to be a hero. Maybe this was his way of doing that. A woman is alive because of him, and in our shared experience, his spirit lives on.

8 TWO PASSENGERS

Seeing the flashing lights up ahead, my fingers reflexively tighten against the leather cover of the steering wheel. A sigh escapes my throat as I prepare myself for what inevitably will be an ugly scene. Motorcycle accidents on this road are almost always bad, and the extent of the injuries can unsettle even the strongest of stomachs.

When dispatch calls me out, everyone knows it's for one purpose… dealing with death. A coroner is a thankless job. That is to be expected, though. Who is truly happy to see the guy who will take away the body of a loved one?

Taking a final breath, I grab my

clipboard and step out into the evening air. The hottest part of the day has passed, but the air still carries much of the heat. I'll be happy to get this over with and back into the air-conditioned vehicle.

I weave my way through a group of black and whites along with an ambulance. Most of the responding units will leave once I take possession of the body. You can see a visible exhale from the people around me, knowing their part of this ugly scene is almost over. *Lucky bastards.*

In front of me, a small circle of people surround the black shroud that has been placed over the deceased. A male and female officer part in order for me to kneel next to the body. I close my eyes and prepare myself for the worst as I do my best to breathe through my mouth in hopes of not catching a whiff of the already pungent body.

I lift one corner of the tarp and cringe

at the sight. Half of the face is covered with deep scratches, but it is the other side that forces me to swallow back the lunch I regret eating just an hour before. The rough surface of the road has ground away a third of his skull. By the time I was done with my assessment, I had identified four other injuries that could have been the reason for death. The chances of survival in this man's case were zero.

I fill out the forms and recruit the paramedics to help me place the body in a bag. Neither one of them are happy about it, but they usually are the ones who do this. I transfer the body onto a gurney and into the car and get the officer in charge of the scene to sign over custody of the body to me.

All i's dotted and t's crossed, I start making my way back to the morgue where I'll drop the body of the deceased off. After that, I'm going home for the night.

I'm driving down the road when my eyes happen to glance in the rearview mirror, and my eyes widen in shock. There's a person sitting in the back of my vehicle staring at the body. I nearly slammed on the brakes in surprise, but I managed simply to pull over to the side of the road and put it in park.

Just to make sure I wasn't seeing things, I looked in the mirror once more. The area in the back is dark enough that I can only make out a silhouette, but he's still there, just staring down at the body bag.

What kind of person sneaks into the back of a coroner's car and stares at a dead body?

The thought sends a shiver running up and down my spine. Obviously, there is something seriously off about this individual, and confronting him might not be the best idea. I briefly considered calling one of the police units at the scene but decided I could probably handle this situation on my own.

I flick on the light in the back so that I can get a look at the person. I can only see one side of his face, but what I can see is pretty beat up. This guy needs a hospital and fast. There is something about him, though, that tickles something in the back of my mind, something familiar about him...

Slowly he turns his head towards me, and I fling myself back in fear. Now that he faces me, I can see that nearly half of his head is missing, and a lightbulb goes on in my brain. The guy sitting in the back of my car is the one that is in the body bag, but somehow, he is sitting up. I know what I'm seeing is impossible, but there it is.

"Hold on, I'm coming. Don't move."

The first thing I should have done was call an ambulance, but I wasn't thinking straight in my shocked state. I just wanted to get to the back to check on the guy. I tore out the door and skidded on the sand as I ran around to the back. I threw open the doors, not sure what I expected to see. The last thing I expected was what I actually saw, nothing. The back of the vehicle was empty except the bag, which still contained the motorcyclist's body.

The back of the truck is kept cold by an air conditioner to slow decomposition, but I'd never felt it this cold before. It felt like a freezer back there. The space isn't very big, but I took a full five minutes looking through every place that I thought a person could hide, but I came up empty, even after double-checking everything twice.

As much as I hated to do it, I had one final thing to check. I grabbed hold of the zipper and undid the seal on the bag. Fluids had begun to fill the bottom of the airtight plastic around the body, but it was obvious that this guy hadn't moved. I zipped up the bag sealing away the gruesome scene within, and shook my head. Nothing was making sense; I knew what I had seen.

I drug my feet making my way back to the front of the truck, trying to reconcile what had just happened. I went through every rational possibility first: stress, lack of sleep, imagination running wild... None of those things felt right, though, like trying to put a square peg in a round hole. A word felt like it was scratching at the back of my brain, but I refused to give it any credence. *Ghost.*

I am a man of science, someone who believes in things that can be seen and proven. And even though I was sure I'd seen the man back there, accepting that it was his spirit was difficult for me. The problem was it just *felt* right. That this was the truth of things.

To this day, I still don't know what to believe about that day. Was it a ghost, or was it my mind creating something that wasn't there? I'm just not sure.

9 INHUMAN

About ten years ago, during which time I was a 911 call-taker, I received one of the creepiest and most unsettling calls I'd ever had. It was the middle of winter and it was freezing that night, cold enough to cover all the windows in frost. Nights like this usually resulted in a calmer, quieter shift since even criminals were reluctant to face the cold weather.

Around three in the morning, my call box turned green, and as usual, I answered asking what the emergency was.

A man began frantically screaming down the phone at me, telling me that his sister was possessed by a demon, and had tried to cut his heart out while he slept. At first I couldn't make sense of his story, thinking I must have misheard, and asked him to slow down and tell me what exactly had happened.

He was panting heavily, and I could hear the fear in his voice as he told me that he'd managed to escape when the attack had started and had locked himself in the bathroom, which was where he was as he was talking to me. He was adamant in his story that his sister had been possessed by a demon and had tried to kill him while he was asleep. I was sure this man was suffering from some kind of psychological issue, but while he was speaking to me, I could hear what sounded like scratching and banging on the door in the background, like something was trying to get into the bathroom where he was hiding.

"There is a demon in my sister's body," he told me in a frantic whisper, while those horrible scratching noises continued. "It's been battling me for days, and tonight it finally got free from its chains…"

While I was struggling to comprehend this man's story, what I heard next chilled me to the core, and still terrifies me to this day. A voice that can only be described as inhuman began taunting the caller through the bathroom door. It didn't sound like the 20-something woman he was claiming her to be. This voice was low and guttural, like her throat had been cut to shreds by razor blades before speaking. I couldn't understand what she was saying, but it didn't sound like any language I'd heard before.

She continued to growl and scream as she banged against the door, while the man on the phone begged me to help him. I'd already dispatched officers to the address he'd given, but they were still a few minutes away. That's when I heard the sound of wood splintering, and the man's wailing grew more frantic. He told me that she was breaking through the door, with her bare fists. I tried to calm him down, but at this point, even I was getting flustered and scared by the noises on the other end of the phone. It sounded more akin to an animal attack rather than something a human could do.

When the police finally arrived, the man's sister let out an ear-piercing scream before the line completely cut off, going dead. I tried to call the number back, but it wouldn't go through, and I was left with more questions than answers about what was going on.

I was shaking when I put down the headset. Usually, when a call was over, I no longer got involved in the case. But this time, I had to know what had happened, if the caller had made it out alright. I'd heard the police arrive, but nothing after that.

My supervisor had been listening to the call as it was happening in real time too, and even they [he/she] were pale and speechless when the line abruptly ended with that terrifying scream. Neither of us knew what had really happened. It wasn't until the end of my shift that I found out. My commanding officer called me into his office to let me know what they'd found when they'd reached the house. He admitted himself that the case would probably give him nightmares for the rest of his life.

It turned out that the man on the phone had been telling the truth about his sister breaking out of her chains. When the officers reached the scene, they had found a young woman with bloody handcuffs around her wrists, a chain still attached to one from where she'd broken free of the restraints. Her whole body had been covered in scratches and bruises that were clearly self-inflicted, due to the blood and skin particles under her nails, and one of her eyes had popped a blood vessel, leaving it bright red. Most of her clothes had been shredded with scratches, and her skin was so pale she looked like she'd been drained of her blood. Whatever she'd gone through wasn't natural, and she needed some serious help.

She was taken in for a psych consultation shortly after and, as you can probably guess, she ended up staying there for a long time. Her brother – the caller – ended up being okay except for some deep gouges in his chest. His sister really had tried to cut his heart out while he'd been asleep, for reasons beyond any of us knew.

There was some talk about arresting the brother, but it was never really clear how complicit he was in his sister's condition, and so nothing ever came of it.

To this day, I still remember that bone-chilling voice as though I'd taken the call yesterday, and it makes me blood run cold every time.

10 THE SILENT OFFICER

I heard this story from one of my young junior officers. She came into work one day looking unsettled about something, and when I asked her if anything was wrong, she confided in me about a strange experience she'd had a few days before.

It was late by the time she had finished her shift. The clock on the wall read a little past two in the morning, and the station was quiet. Most of the other officers on her shift had already clocked out, and as she walked past the admin offices on her way to the locker room, she noticed it was empty inside. One of the desk lamps was flickering faintly in the corner, but she left it on for the sallow yellow glow it emitted out into the corridor. The station could get eerily dark at night, with shadows seeming thicker and more abundant than normal.

As she neared the end of the hallway, she began to hear footsteps echoing faintly behind her. She paused, wondering if she was imagining it. But amidst the silence, there was the distinct clatter of shoes against lino, echoing down the hallway towards her. The sound seemed displaced, she'd told me, as though it didn't quite belong.

Curious, she turned around, half-expecting to see another officer behind her. But there was nobody else there. The air in the corridor was colder than usual, and she could feel a slight chill creeping along her arms and neck. She got a distinct feeling that she wasn't alone.

Shrugging it off, she was about to keep going when she heard something else. A quiet mutter, or a whisper, alighting the air behind her.

She froze, wondering if someone else was on the same floor. Driven by curiosity and a dawning trepidation, she ended up going back the way she had come, if only to ease her suspicions and put her mind at rest.

As she was passing the admin office again, a shadow caught her eye. Someone was stood by one of the desks in the corner, where the lamp was flickering and humming faintly.

She peered inside, and sure enough, there was a man stood there, dressed in the standard police uniform. He didn't look up when she entered, but she could see enough of his face to know that she didn't recognize him.

"Oh, hello," she said, slightly disconcerted at the fact she hadn't noticed him before. She stepped further into the room, glancing vaguely around to see if there was another door. "I didn't realize there was anyone up here."

The man said nothing in return. He was staring down at the desk, his features cast in shadow. He kept silent the whole time as though he hadn't noticed her. Thinking he might want to be left alone, the young officer excused herself without saying anything further and slipped back out of the room.

However, something urged her to glance back, and she saw with sudden alarm that the man was no longer there. She blinked furiously, rubbing her eyes, but it was clear there was nobody in the room.

At this point, she thought she must be imagining things. It was late, and it had been a long shift. It could have been nothing but a hallucination conjured from a tired mind. But it still creeped her out, and she ended up jogging the rest of the way to the locker room, glancing every now and then over her shoulder.

She saw nothing else that night other than a couple of faulty lights in the foyer.

Then, a couple of days later, with the incident still on her mind, she noticed a familiar face on the wall of fallen officers. A picture of the same officer she had seen that night was among them.

That's where I found her: staring at the picture with a look of puzzlement and disconcertment on her face. When I asked her if something was wrong, she pointed to the officer and asked who he was.

I explained that he was an officer who had killed himself with his own service weapon a couple of years ago. As I thought about it, I realized it must have been around a similar date as it was then, during the second week of April. When I told her that the officer was dead, she blanched suddenly and explained everything she'd seen.

I told her that his desk used to be the one in the corner of the office, exactly where she had seen him standing. Some of the other officers reported getting a 'bad vibe' from the area, and the light on the desk was constantly flickering, despite changing the bulb, but nobody had ever seen anything.

I assured the officer it was nothing to worry about, but I kept turning the story over in my mind, wondering if what she'd seen was real.

I had never gotten a chance to know the officer properly, since our department was large, and we didn't work in the same area. But in the few dealings I'd had with him, he'd seemed like a very talented and intelligent individual who had a clear passion for the work he did here. It was a huge shock and a great loss to the department when we found out he'd killed himself. None of us ever really saw it coming in the days leading up to it.

Now when I'm near the admin offices, I sometimes look out for the flickering lamp or listen out for footsteps that shouldn't be there. On occasion, I think I catch a shadow moving out of the corner of my eye, but I could just be seeing things. I do find it somewhat comforting that he still hangs around his old desk, almost as though he couldn't leave this place behind. Maybe he's watching over us, making sure we all keep out of trouble. Or maybe this was the one place he felt happy. Who really knows?

11 THE HILL

It must have been nearing 2:00 in the morning. I was sitting in an unmarked vehicle in the flat of a hill, just off the highway, monitoring the early-morning traffic. The area was notorious for drivers going 15-20mph over the speed limit because of the long stretch of straight road, so it was a prime spot for flagging down lawbreakers. Despite that, most officers at my department expressed a certain reluctance to sit here. The hill where I was parked had something of a reputation in the local area due to being a crime scene almost twenty-six years previous. The body of a murder victim was discovered on the hill, but the case was never solved due to lack of evidence and a positive identification of the victim. Hyped up by the local media, no doubt, the area was long suspected of being 'haunted'. People reported feeling nauseous or dizzy when hanging around the hill, and even the officers had bought into it, refusing to be stationed here. I didn't really believe in that kind of thing, so it didn't bother me when I was assigned this spot for traffic monitoring.

As I was sitting there, keeping an eye on the horizon for any oncoming headlights, something drew my attention. A shadow had just passed across the back of my unit, coming round from the passenger side. I blinked a couple of times, clearing the haze from my eyes from staring into the distance for too long, wondering if I was seeing things. But then I saw the shadow cross over to the driver's side, moving across the front of the vehicle.

Other than the pale glimmer of the moon, there were no lights on the highway. The road was shrouded completely in darkness, making it impossible to see if there was anything there that could have cast a shadow.

That's when I heard footsteps too. It was only faint, but it sounded like grass crunching softy beneath someone's shoes, to the left of the vehicle.

I squinted through the window, but I still couldn't see anything beyond the gloom.

Thinking there was somebody outside the car, I started up the ignition and switched on my headlights, casting a dazzling glare across the grass in front.

With the whole area lit up, I looked out of each window to see who was out there. There was nobody. The shadow had been too large to be an animal, but there was nowhere out here for a person to hide. The hill was completely empty.

I began to feel somewhat unsettled by the thought there might be someone out there, walking around my car. It must have just been my imagination that conjured those shadows, but somehow, I felt convinced I wasn't alone.

Shaking my head, I flicked off my headlights and settled back in my seat. I kept my hazard lights on, casting an eerie red glow around the car, just in case anything was out there.

The road itself had gone unusually quiet. Although it was the early hours of the morning, there were usually still cars on the highway at this time. Yet, I could barely see the glimmer of a high beam in the distance.

The wind began to pick up outside, making the unit rock slightly. The grasses on the hill began to sway, creating anomalies in the shadows.

I forced myself to keep my eyes on the road, watching the horizon. Unease gnawed at my stomach.

Something moved past the car, a shadow darting across my periphery.

My heart jumped, and I reflexively switched the headlights back on, flooding the hill.

There was nobody out there. No movement but the wind rustling through the grass.

I decided it was time to leave. There hadn't been a car driving past in some time, and I was starting to spook myself out. There wasn't much point in hanging around anyway, especially since my shift was coming to an end.

As I set the car into motion and drove onto the highway, I flicked a glance up to the rear-view mirror. For a moment, my blood went cold. It looked as though there was someone standing in the shadow of the hill, watching me drive away. I quickly dragged my eyes back to the road, scolding myself for being silly. I was letting those stories get to me. That was all.

I didn't stop feeling uneasy until I reached the next town, where the streets were well-lit, and there was more traffic on the road. It was then that something blinked on my dashboard: the security camera. I pulled over to the side of the road and took the camera down from its hook. It must have been recording since I hit my emergency lights, which meant if there had been someone out there on the hill, the camera would have caught it.

I rewound the footage to where it began recording and hit play, my heart thumping with nervous anticipation.

I hadn't imagined the shadow after all. The video clearly showed a figure walking around the car, starting from the passengers' side of the vehicle before moving around to the drivers' side. Then, for about half a second after, the entire video went black. It was almost as though someone had put their finger over the lens, smudging the visual. After that, it went back to normal, and there was no longer a shadow in view. I wound the tape forward a few more minutes, but the shadowy figure didn't return.

I set down the camera, unease settling in the pit of my stomach as I wondered what it could have been.

The shadow had no visual features, nothing to suggest it was a person, but what else could it have been?

I tried not to dwell on it as I drove back to the station. Maybe I just needed some rest, and the whole thing would seem silly in the morning.

Nevertheless, the next time I was asked to go to the hill to monitor traffic, I refused.

12 ALARMING

As a police officer, I often blame a particularly busy or crazy night on a full moon or some other natural event that Old Wives will swear invoke abnormal behavior. (Don't even get me started on Halloween. Just the whole month of October in general, I am not even going to go there.) Truthfully, I never put much stock in old superstitions, but it helps combat the struggle of dealing with chaos on those nights when it seems the world has lost its mind. A light-hearted twist on human behavior, if you will. But as far as whole-heartedly trusting in the supernatural, no, that was not me. Not until one night in late June.

My partner and I were seven hours into a twelve-hour shift, sitting in the cruiser and finishing another chilled cup of bad coffee. It had been an uneventful evening. I couldn't tell you why, but I vividly remember looking up into the sky and thinking about how empty it was. You live or work in the city long enough, and you get used to the starless nights, but there were no clouds, no fog, and no moon, just an empty black expanse of sky. Anyway, I don't know why I remember this in such great detail, but I do, and it unexplainably gives me the creeps even still.

We were in an area of development that night. New buildings and refurbished buildings were all up and down the street. Construction was everywhere. Which meant vandalism in this area was likely and happened often. We had just finished what passed for coffee and a meal when dispatch sent out an alert. One of those remote security companies had called 911, alerting police that an alarm, possibly an intruder, had been set off in the upper levels of a nearby office building. We were only about a block away. We let dispatch know we would be responding to the call.

"Copy that, Officer. I will let the caller know a unit is responding." Dispatch clicked off.

"On our way." My partner spoke into the radio.

"Officers, the caller has informed you they are contacting a key holder. Please wait for key holder's access before entering premises." Dispatch clicked off once more, and my partner radioed a quick response of acknowledgment.

"I sure hope the intruder waited for the key holder before heading inside." My partner rolled his eyes.

"Oh, I'm sure they did. Everyone knows manners first and all that." The deadpan that night was heavy in the air. It had been an incredibly quiet and slow shift.

Arriving at the given address, we got out of the cruiser and assessed quickly there didn't seem to be any obvious signs of a break-in. The refurbished building, according to what I had heard and what the offices listed on the newly installed sign said, it housed mostly doctor's offices and a pharmacy. According to the information we had been told, the alarm had been triggered in one of the empty upstairs offices. We both continued to look around the building as we waited for the key holder to arrive. Inside, the building was completely dark. There did not appear to be any lights on inside at all. We walked around the building and never saw any signs of a break-in or a disturbance of any sort. Coming back around to the front of the building, there was a man waiting by the front door.

He was of average height, looked to be middle-aged with thick, greying chestnut hair that was parted to the side and a neatly trimmed beard. He had brown, forgettable eyes and wore slacks and a dark button-up shirt. He seemed to be the kind of guy anyone could describe and yet was so memorable as to be utterly unrecognizable. He could have been anyone, anywhere. He was friendly enough, however, especially given the late hour. He held a keyring in his right hand and waved to us as we walked up to him with his left. "Good evening, sir." My partner and I both greeted him.

"Good evening, officers." And without further prompting, he turned and unlocked the office building doors. He strode over to a switch behind the reception desk and flipped on a few of the lobby lights. "The alarm was triggered on the top floor. The empty offices up there." He leaned against the desk. To the left was the elevator, and to the right, the stairs. We first opted to take the stairs, but the door marking them as such was locked.

"Do you mind opening this up for us, please, sir?" I asked the man.

He continued to lean against the desk. He hadn't moved since he parked himself there.

"Don't have the key to that door. The elevator should work." He said, his back to us. I looked at my partner to confirm that this was strange. Judging by the questioning look on his face, he agreed. We walked around to the other side of the desk and hit the up arrow. The elevator dinged and opened immediately. I glanced over at the man. He was still standing there staring out the front windows as though he was lost in thought and completely alone. Weird.

Inside the elevator, I began to get a weird feeling, but I just chalked it up to too much caffeine and the interaction with the key holder. "Doesn't seem like this is turning into anything at all. Probably just a fault in the security system. Or a mouse." My partner is not a small man. In fact, the last time he was described as small was likely when he was in kindergarten. He spends his free time at the gym and is all around, just a scary looking dude. He is a great officer, though, and I have always appreciated having him at my back. While a nice reprieve from the chaos, calls like this were boring and not what he wanted to be doing.

"Probably. But we still have to check it out. You never know." The elevator dinged open to reveal another waiting room lobby area. This top floor was completely dark except for a minuscule amount of light coming from the only hallway. At first, I thought it was just light coming from a window at the end, but it couldn't have been that. There was no moon.

We pulled the issued flashlights from our belts and began to do a more thorough search. The waiting room was obviously empty. There was not much to it. Several chairs lined the walls, and two coffee tables sat off-center. The reception desk was empty of anything and everything. This floor did not appear to be currently in use. We cautiously walked to the darkened hall where all the exam rooms and offices were located. There was a single, flickering, overhead light fading in and out of clarity at the very end of the hallway.

Every horror film I had ever seen came to mind as I looked at that light. My partner, unlike his usual sarcastic self, said nothing as we proceeded down the hall to the first door in the hallway. I checked the knob and found it locked. My partner checked the door directly across from the door I checked. He found it locked as well. Two doors down. Six more to go. We methodically checked each door. And each time, we found it to be locked. The last door to be checked was at the very end of the hall and sketchily illuminated by the ever-flickering overhead light. My heart was pounding in my chest. An irrational fear had settled into my nerves.

My partner checked this last door and expected it to be locked that same as the others. But that was not the case. The knob twisted down and released its hold on the jam, silently gliding into the dark room. Steeling ourselves for confrontation, we took a deep calming breath and entered the room. We examined the room with our flashlights, carefully and scrupulously taking in the details of the abandoned office.

    A simple wooden desk sat directly in front of the shut and locked windows. A calendar from several years ago was still under the protective glass that covered the desktop. A jar of black pens sat on the corner, and a half-used notepad was resting in front of the jar. A tall metal file cabinet was placed in the two back corners of the office. Two doors were side by side to the right of the office. In one, we found nothing. It appeared to be a small coat closet. In the other was a bathroom. Again, nothing in there aside from the toilet and the sink. The office didn't yield any signs of an intruder or that anyone had been in here for years.

"Can you see anything that would indicate why the alarm was triggered?" I asked my partner.

"No. Let's get out of here. It was probably a glitch or something in the system." He was already heading for the door. I followed right behind him and almost plowed into his huge frame as he dead stopped in the doorway. The ever-flickering light was no more. It had gone completely out, but the light above the elevator shone bright and steady. Across from the door we stood in was another door. A door that had been locked tight just a moment before. A door that was now standing wide open.

I heard the swallowed fear as my partner gulped and stepped out into the hall; I was right on his heels. I stepped around to stand beside him and was immediately met with an unnerving sight. Each and every door we had just checked and found to be locked was standing open. Every. Single. One. At this point, training overrode fear and nerves. We began to check inside each of the now opened doors. These were doors to exam rooms. Each one was empty. Not even the exam beds were left inside. We left the doors as we found them – open.

The last door standing open was to another office. This one was empty. No personal bathroom or closet, just an empty desk. Still, we walked inside just to be sure. The moment we were both inside the office, our radios blasted a high-pitched, ear-piercing static that about drove us to our knees. In the hall, we heard a door slam shut with such force I was sure it would have splintered. I can't tell you who was out the door first, but my partner's long legs got him to the elevator first. The doors dinged and opened on the first push of the call button. We were inside and hurriedly pushing the doors close and lobby button.

In the lobby, the elevator let us out without incident. "Where is that keyholder? I have some questions for him." My partner was not having this experience. He was clearly shaken. I know I was too. The keyholder was nowhere to be seen. We walked outside to see if he had stepped out, but he seemed to have vanished.

"He just left us here. What is going on with this place?" I wondered out loud, needing to hear something, even if it was my own voice.

"I'll contact dispatch. Explain what is going on and get the number to the keyholder." He did that, and as I listened to the exchange between him and dispatch, I grew increasingly more uneasy.

"Officer ---, the keyholder should be arriving in five to ten minutes. The security company had difficulties contacting the keyholder on-call." The woman at dispatch was clearly annoyed. She probably thought she was being pranked.

"Dispatch, we have been inside for over twenty minutes. We were just with the guy!" My partner was struggling to keep the calm in his voice.

"That is impossible, Officer. I'm telling you, the keyholder was only reached a few minutes ago. They are still en route to the building." Dispatch clicked off, leaving radio silence. We decided to continue waiting outside for the en route keyholder.

A few minutes later, a small, dark blue car pulled into the parking spot immediately behind our cruiser. It shut off, and out of the driver's door stepped a young woman. She was dressed in jeans and a hoodie and looked like she had just rolled out of bed; clearly bothered to be up and out this late. "Good evening, officers. Sorry about the wait." She said as she came towards us holding a big round keyring.

"Good evening, ma'am. Another keyholder already let us inside. We didn't see any signs of intrusion, tampering, or vandalism. But it does seem like there could be a glitch or malfunction in the system." I explained as she came to a stop in front of where we stood.

"What? I'm the one on call. I am the only one with the building keys right now." She was obviously confused and a little frustrated.

"A man met us here about thirty minutes ago." I went on to describe how he looked and how he left without saying anything. The more I explained, the more the blood drained from her face.

"He sounds a lot like," she paused and looked around uncomfortably, "he sounds a lot like one of the doctors who worked here several years ago. I had just started, but I remember because he committed suicide." Again, she paused, this time crossing her arms, and took a ragged breath, "He jumped out of his office window." Chills shot up my spine. Judging by my partner's reaction, I think the same must have happened to him too.

Neither of us ever told anyone about that call. There was no explanation immediately at my disposal, scientific or superstitious. Supernatural, maybe. But I can't bring myself to dive too deeply into that realm of possibility.

13 FIREHOUSE APPARITIONS

I've resided next to a haunted firehouse for almost seventeen years. It's still in use today as a small holding station for fire engines and equipment, but it isn't in use 24/7 like the bigger stations in town. The firehouse itself is quite old-fashioned and somewhat run-down on the outside; ivy has begun to creep along one side of the bricks, and the windows are dirty with cobwebs and dust, since it isn't a fully maintained building, and it's only ever occupied when a call comes in.

Over the years, I've heard countless stories from locals describing their experiences there, all relating to paranormal happenings and things that cannot be fully explained. I'm not aware of the firehouse's full history, and I can't give you any specific names or stories, but I know that a few members have lost their lives while on the job over the years, and many people believe that some of their spirits are still hanging around.

One woman I spoke to claimed to have seen an apparition. She'd been walking past the firehouse one evening when she felt as though she was being watched, and when she looked up, there was someone standing at the window, staring right at her. There were no active calls at the time, so there shouldn't have been anybody inside. But she was insistent that she had seen a man dressed in an old-fashioned fireman's garb watching her from the uppermost window. She described his stare as intense but not threatening, though the sight of him had definitely unnerved her. The woman had turned away and kept on walking, assuming she was merely imagining things. When she glanced back, the man was already gone, as though he had never been there at all.

Other stories I've heard range from seeing shadowy figures and hearing noises that can't be explained coming from within the firehouse. Since I live right next door, it's pretty easy for me to keep track of when there are people in the building or not, and a majority of the time, these experiences take place when the firehouse is empty, leaving no possible room for explanation.

I've had my own strange experiences too. On more than one occasion, while I've been out gardening in my front yard, I've heard voices spilling out through the firehouse's air conditioning vent, which faces my garden. One time I thought I heard someone crying out for help, but the firehouse was empty at the time, and there was nobody out on the street either. Sometimes I can hear a male voice speaking too, although it's always difficult to make out exactly what he's saying as the voice seems to fade and get louder without reason. I know for a fact that

each time, the house has been empty, and there should be nobody inside speaking loud enough for me to hear them through the vent.
My nephew is a fireman himself, and he too has heard and seen things that he can't explain from the firehouse next door. He told me about the experience he'd had when he'd been inside the station alone one night. The others had all gone home, leaving him to check the equipment and lock up, since he lived right next door and it was his turn to do the usual rounds. He was certain he was alone as he'd watched everyone walk out the door. But as he was about to leave himself, he heard someone humming from deeper inside the firehouse. He thought it odd but assumed it might

have been coming from outside rather than in the building itself. Nevertheless, he decided to check the station again to make sure nobody had come back without him realising. As he approached the locker room, where the sound seemed to be coming from, he saw a shadow disappear through the doorway, as though someone had quickly darted inside. But when he went to check, there was *nobody* there. He told me he'd been pretty spooked at that point, and got the feeling he wasn't alone, even though he was, as far as he could tell. He left as quickly as he could after that. I remember how shaken he seemed when he'd come home, and he told me the story that same night after I wheedled it out of him. I'd already known some of the rumours about the firehouse, so I had no qualms about believing him.

On another occasion, my son and I were out in the yard when we heard a door slam from inside the firehouse, even though the place was, as usual, completely empty. He ran to go and see who it was, thinking there might have been an emergency or one of the other guys had gone in, but there was nobody there, and the door was locked, meaning there couldn't have been anyone inside either. Neither of us could find an explanation for it, just like we couldn't really explain a lot of things we saw happen over there. Some of the other firemen and women have claimed to see doors opening and closing on their own, have glimpsed shadowy figures that seem to disappear into thin air, and have heard footsteps in the building even when they're the only ones there. The number of different witnesses and accounts that have stemmed from the firehouse over the years only goes to show how haunted the place truly is. Given how dangerous the job is and how many lives have been lost over the years since it was built, I suppose it's no surprise that spirits still linger around the old building.

Even my son, a brave fireman, is now too afraid to go into the firehouse alone, especially on a night, after the strange things he has witnessed. So are most of the others he works with, who have also experienced unexplainable things while staying there after dark. They make it a point now to never lock up or leave someone there alone, especially when it's already gone dark.

14 LONG FORGOTTEN

My uncle works as a dispatcher in my town, and he recently told my family and me about one of the weirdest calls he's ever gotten in the whole of his career. I have to admit, after he told me about it, I couldn't stop thinking about it for days afterwards, and it still freaks me out when I remember it.

It was fairly late at night, maybe between 11pm to midnight, when he received a call from a local landline number. When he answered it, however, there was only static on the other end, as though the connection hadn't fully gone through. After unsuccessfully trying to reach out to the person on the other side of the line, the call cut off and he assumed it had merely been a mistake or a prank. Over the next hour, however, the same thing happened another two times. There wasn't anything wrong on his end, since he'd received calls in between that had gone through perfectly fine. But the same landline called three times, and every time he answered, he was met with nothing but crackling static. There wasn't even the semblance of a voice on the other side, just plain white noise. Once things had quietened down, he eventually called a squad to go and check the address, which he'd managed to trace from the caller ID. The fact that they had attempted to call three times suggested that there might actually be an emergency, but for some reason the caller had been unable to get through.

It was only afterwards that he heard about what came of the call from the landline, and the squad that he sent there. And it's a story that has bothered him ever since.

According to one of the officers who were dispatched to investigate the call, the house was seemingly unoccupied when they first got there. None of the lights were switched on, the curtains were drawn, and all of the doors and windows were locked. Nobody answered from inside, no matter how many times they knocked and announced their presence. Thinking something might have happened to incapacitate the caller, they made the decision to break the door open and force their way into the building.

Once they were in, the first thing they noticed was the smell. The heavy, rotting stench of something that had died long ago.

From their initial observation, the place had been untouched for a while. A thick layer of dust caked every surface, and one of the officers was sure he'd heard rats scuttling in the walls as they'd searched the house. The place stunk of damp and mildew, but it was nothing compared to the horrible smell of a decaying corpse. They would have thought the house completely vacant if not for that smell.

They found the body in the living room, sitting in an old leather armchair that was also caked in dust and grime.

Covering his nose to ward off the stench, the officer had used his flashlight to inspect the body. Although it was heavily decomposed, he was able to determine that it was a man somewhere in his mid to late eighties. He seemed to have died from natural causes judging from their preliminary examination, as there was no sign of any external injuries or wounds. The coroner was later able to clarify that he'd died of a heart attack while sitting in his chair, and no foul play had been involved. They immediately requested an ambulance to take the body away, although it was clear he'd been dead for a while. They found out afterwards that the man had actually been dead for over five months, steadily wasting away in the darkness of his own home. Nobody had checked up on him or called the police during that time to express concern about him, and after a brief investigation, it was found that he had no family left alive. He'd died alone and forgotten about.

That isn't the strangest or most disturbing part of the story, however, because the question still remained: who had called dispatch? Someone must have placed the call, and the landline phone responsible had been traced to the inside of the house. Yet when the police did a full sweep of the house, they found nobody else there. There wasn't a single footprint or mark in the dust to suggest anybody had been in the house recently either. And there was no way anyone could have left after placing the call, since all the doors and windows were locked from the inside. The only other person who could have called for help was the dead man. Which, of course, was impossible.

What bothered the officer even more was the fact that the house had no running electricity. It turned out that all of the utilities in the house had been shut off when the resident had stopped paying the bills, after his death. Nothing worked, and nor had it worked for a long time. The landline had no way of operating, and yet somehow it had been used to place a call to the police.

The phone itself had been found in the hallway, still plugged in. But when the officer picked up the receiver, there wasn't a dial tone on the other end, and nothing happened when he tried punching a number into the dial pad. The phone was completely dead. Nor had it been disturbed recently. When they dusted for fingerprints, there was nothing to be found.

It was almost as though a call had never been placed, but the record existed in the dispatcher's files, and it had brought those officers to that very house where the dead man was.

It remains a mystery to this day who had placed the call and how they had managed it without a working phone. But in the end, who knows how long that dead body would have stayed there if they hadn't. Maybe that's all that really matters.

15 DUMMY

My mom was a 911 dispatcher back in the 90s. I was around seven years old at the time, but when I got older and more curious, I started asking her about some of the calls that she could still recall from that time. She told me about one in particular that was really bad, and still makes her feel terribly uneasy when she thinks about it.

She was working one year on the night of Halloween. She told me that Halloween tended to be one of the busiest nights for police and ambulance services, since many people took it as an opportunity to be more reckless and dangerous than any other night of the year. She'd taken a lot of calls already that night, but this one stuck out the most.

It was around 10 or 11pm when a call came in from a young woman. When my mom asked what the emergency was, she explained that there were a couple of guys driving around town with some kind of dummy or mannequin dragging behind their truck. The dummy itself was falling apart as it was dragged over the tarmac, and pieces of clothing and chunks of plastic were being torn off and scattered all over the roads of the city. It wasn't doing any harm as it was, but there was a risk that the dummy could fall off and cause an accident, plus the woman said that the sight was rather gruesome in the dark and might cause some disturbances if others saw it.

Given that it was Halloween, the most likely explanation was that the whole thing was a prank, since it was exactly the kind of thing that kids would use to scare people for a joke. My mom made a note of the incident, but there were more urgent calls to attend to first, so she didn't act on it right away. As the night went on, however, more and more calls started coming in about the truck dragging along this disintegrating dummy all around the city. It seemed to be upsetting people quite a bit, so she eventually sent out a patrol car to try and find the truck and put an end to the charade.

As they were driving around, looking for the truck, the police officers came across several articles of clothing and bits of plastic that had fallen off, but no sign of the dummy itself. When they eventually managed to catch up to the truck down and flag it down, they made a horrifying discovery.

The dummy turned out to not be a dummy at all. It was a person. A dead body, to be exact.

The guys driving the truck claimed to be completely ignorant of the body stuck to the back of their truck, and after some questioning and retracing their activities of the night, the truth was finally revealed, and it was worse than anyone could have realised.

The two guys had gone to a store earlier that evening to pick up some alcohol and snacks for the rest of the night. As they left, they had unknowingly backed the truck into an elderly man who had been standing behind them in their blind spot. Somehow, the man's clothing had gotten caught on the truck's rear bumper, and when they'd drove off, they'd taken the man with them. These two men never even knew that they had been driving around in their truck, dragging this old man's body around town for miles, while people who saw it merely thought they were towing along a plastic dummy.

I can't even imagine what kind of pain that poor man had gone through in the moments before he died, unable to claw himself free from the back of the truck as he was dragged over the tarmac at horrifying speeds. Those pieces of clothing and plastic that people thought had belonged to a dummy were actually the clothing, flesh and body parts of that old man, being scattered around the whole city. When they finally got him free, his body had been in a gruesome state, completely and irrevocably broken. It must have been a horrible job for the officers who had to go back and find all of the pieces of him on the streets and the road.

Just thinking about it still gives me chills, and my mom told me it was one of the worst calls she'd ever taken when she found out what had happened afterwards. Nothing like that had ever happened to her since.

But the story doesn't end there. What's even weirder is that, when the paramedics arrived to attend to what was left of the man's body, one of them claimed to see an elderly man standing by the truck, just watching them. It was dark and they were unable to see who it was, but the figure turned and walked off into the field by the side of the road and seemed to just disappear into thin air. Nobody knew who the man was, but it almost seemed as though he had been waiting there until the paramedics came, and then he'd simply… vanished.

Given the amount of damage his body sustained throughout the whole ordeal, the man was proclaimed DOA (dead on arrival) at the hospital, and the two guys riding the truck were arrested and convicted of involuntary manslaughter.

16   B & E

Glowing computer screens illuminated the ceiling of the video surveillance room above me. I rub my eyes trying to wipe away the fatigue and boredom that had inevitably set in after the first six hours of my twelve-hour shift. A low-grade headache had set in behind my eyes and was threatening to grow into a full-on migraine making every screen a little explosion of pain.

Something between a sigh and a moan escapes me as I think not for the first time the government was paying me to do nothing. In the six years I had been employed here, not one interesting thing had passed across the screens in front of me. Sure, there were stories from the past, tales of legend that based on my experience seemed more on par with someone telling you they'd seen bigfoot once instead of a guy trying to jump the fence. Still the pay was good, and it came with benefits.

Looking down at my phone to see if I had missed a call or a text. The screen simply displayed the time along with the few apps I kept on the desktop that I used regularly to pass the time. Like the building I was in, nobody seemed interested in chatting. I could make the first move, text someone in hopes of sparking a conversation, but why bother? No one was really awake at midnight and those that were had better things to do than shoot the breeze.

My eyes pan across the small pictures in front of me as I try to see anything out of the ordinary. There are motion detectors that would alert me to anything or anyone that shouldn't be there, but I had to make sure.

One by one I gaze at the pictures, they are clear video but with no motion they look like digital photographs. Every few of them I have to squeeze my eyes shut, trying to give them a break trying to spare myself the worst of the pain.

About halfway through the group of cameras something catches my eye. A large white blob seems to be floating around one of the restricted access areas of the building. I checked the map to see if one of the detectors had gone off, but there didn't appear to be anything out of the ordinary.

I figured a moth, or some other bug had made its way onto the lens of the camera and was blocking the view. I pushed a few buttons and moved the rollerball that controlled the 360° camera view hoping to scare off the nuisance bug.

The camera slowly panned back and forth then up and down. The white blob moved out of view but when I would come back to the preferred frame it would still be there.

Confused I brought the image up on the main screen so I could get a better view of what I was looking at. So far whatever it was hadn't appeared to move so I thought maybe it could be a reflection from one of the lights in there, but the computer told me that all lights were off in that part of the building.

I turned a dial to zoom in, bringing the strange white cloud full screen on the monitor. It didn't seem to have any real form on top, but below it two columns appeared to be going down to the floor, almost like it had legs and was standing there.

Different thoughts started swirling in my head. I'm definitely not a skeptic when it comes to paranormal activities, but now, being faced with this, I tried to explain away the possibility. It just had to be something simple that I hadn't thought of. I'm not supposed to leave for very long, but I felt it prudent to go check out the area to make sure everything was as it should be.

The room in question was only about thirty seconds from my post and the only exit would take them right into my path. If someone was there, I would know soon, and if not... well then, I'd cross that bridge when I got there.

I grab my flashlight and put my key into the lock ready to turn it and take whoever might be inside by surprise. I steady myself, turn the key and twist the handle.

My light sweeps back and forth, illuminating every corner of the room one by one then settles in the center. Nothing, absolutely nothing. My hand fumbles against the wall for a second before I find the light switch but when I do there is no doubt, other than the desks and cabinets I'm alone.

From where I stand the camera appears okay, but I make a mental note to have maintenance check it when they are next here. I flip off the lights and close the door so I can return to my post.

In the short trip back I my mind wouldn't let the issue rest. Instead of getting closure and a sense of relief I was left with more questions. Something had to of caused the image on the screen, but what?

When I got back, I rewound the playback of the room. The white cloud was still there and then it wasn't. All of a sudden it disappeared from view as if it had never been there. A matter of seconds after it vanished, I saw myself come in and turn on the lights. It was almost like it had known I was coming and ran off before I could come in contact with it.

A few days later maintenance gave the camera a once over and determined that it was functioning normally. After which I no longer had any doubt of what I had seen.

17 DISPATCH

Night had fallen hours ago yet I still had more than half of my shift remaining. My eyelids were already starting to feel heavy, and I was starting to get concerned that I wouldn't be able to make it. Thankfully, a loud beep comes through my headset alerting me to an incoming call.

After sending the appropriate units to the scene I logged the information into the computer and made myself ready for another call to come in. Some movement out of the corner of my eye catches my attention and I notice an officer standing near one of the doors down the hall. Even this time of night this isn't something out of the ordinary. People from stations all over the city will come to dispatch to pick up supplies and I just assumed this was the case here.

Another call came in and I went back to work, still, I kept my eye out to see if the officer down the hall someone was, I knew. The only exit in this area would take them right past my desk so I was sure to get a good look at them.

The call took me a little over 15 minutes to complete and document during which the unknown officer never walked by. Either he had a huge order to fill or didn't know the lay of the room. Wanting to do my best to be of help, I told my supervising officer I was going to see if the officer at the end of the hall needed any help. He gave me a little bit of a weird look but didn't say anything when I left.

The hall was empty when I arrived, so I assumed he was still inside. When I opened the door, I was surprised to find that the lights were off. *Why would someone not turn on the lights?*

I flipped the switch and the florescent tubes beamed to life. "Hello? Are you in here?" No one answered my call so I decided to explore the few isles to see if I could find him.

I walked down the front row, looking down each isle I passed expecting to see someone. Even when I reached the end of the hall I turned around and checked again expecting that somehow, I had just missed them somehow even though I knew the likelihood of that was almost none. Besides, the room was quiet except for my own footsteps, I was sure that any sound besides my own would have stood out.

With a last look back over my shoulder I shrugged and flicked off the lights. Before I could take a single step, a hard push came from behind me. The blow was hard enough to send me sprawling forward and crashing to the floor in a heap.

I spun around and tried to get a look at the culprit that had done this to me, but the door was already shut. One of the other dispatchers had seen me go down and had rushed to my side to make sure I was okay. I wasn't hurt, but something made me hold my tongue when it came to telling him about the push I felt. I had been sure no one was behind me, but there was no doubt in my mind that it hadn't just been a clumsy moment. Someone or something had caused me to fall, but what would they say if they couldn't find someone there? I could be forced to endure an embarrassing psychological evaluation and then there would be the whispers about me being the crazy lady that was convinced a ghost had attacked her.

I picked myself up off the ground and despite my fellow officer's offers of assistance I assured him that I was okay. "By the way, did you see what happened to that guy who was standing down by the storage room earlier? I didn't recognize him and must have missed him when he went by."

He gave me a strange look, not dissimilar from the one my supervisor had made. "Um, the only person that has been over here the entire night is you."

My face twisted into a look of frustration. "What are you talking about? He was right there just a few minutes ago..."

He shook his head. "You must have hit your head or something, I'm telling you there was no one there."

I knew there were security cameras in the hall and was getting tired of the argument. "Come on, I'll show you." We walked over to the supervising officer's desk and asked him to pull up the video footage. He probably assumed we wanted to watch me fall and didn't argue. He continued to rewind the video, and to my sunrise the only thing it had picked up the entire time was me walking into the supply room and then flopping out onto the ground.

The man I had seen was nowhere to be seen.

18 RIDE ALONG

Over and over again I pressed down hard on her chest trying to force the blood through her body. The heart monitor was screaming at me because it couldn't find a pulse. I wanted to yell and tell it to shut up, that I knew she was in trouble and didn't need it telling me. At that moment it was all I could do to keep up with the 120 compressions a minute pace I was trying to set.

I braced myself as we turned the final corner before the hospital, and I felt the ambulance pick up speed. "Come on, we have to hurry! She isn't going to make it!" I yell to the driver. The only response I get from him is a quick look at his eyes in the mirror, they're worried eyes, probably the same one's I have.

What I'm doing isn't working. I know I have to get her heart beating. I went to try the defibrillator but like the compressions I wasn't getting any results. About the time I'm reaching for the epinephrine, the entire truck rocks as we hit the entrance to the hospital.

"We're here! Get ready to offload!" The driver yells at me.

From there things go very quickly. After about a minute the woman is in the hands of the doctors and nurses that will try to save her life. I already know that she is gone, even if they do manage to bring her back, the likelihood of her having no long-term effects is almost none. The thought weighs heavy in my head as I walk back outside.

I hate nights like this one...

Me and my partner's walk back to the ambulance is silent. I'd been doing this long enough to know what the outcome would be. The best thing that can happen now is to get the next call so we can turn the page.

I climb in the driver's side door trying to shut out the image of the woman's and her vacant eyes staring at me. For some reason I just don't seem to be able to shake it.

Unconsciously my eyes find the handset of the radio, trying to will the dispatcher's voice from the small plastic box. When I realize what I'm asking for I shake my head in an attempt to clear it.

Am I really hoping for someone to get hurt... "Come on man, pull yourself together."

The response gets my partner's attention. "What are you talking about?"

I rack my brain trying to come up with something that makes sense. "Sorry, I just thinking out loud." His eyes linger on me for a few seconds, and I feel him weighing the truth of my words. I'm rescued further scrutiny when the dispatcher's voice booms from the radio.

There is a major traffic accident reported and we are needed to transport one of the drivers to the hospital. Some nights I wish the radio would shut up and give me a few minutes to just breathe, now though, I've never been happier for the distraction.

The ambulance is in gear and we're moving in a matter of seconds, lights and siren on. Determined to have a better result I push the vehicle faster than is normally safe. My hands threaten to crush the wheel squeezing it with anxiety fueled strength. The two of us barreling down the street more than 20 MPH above the speed limit, missing other vehicles at times by only a foot.

We are at the halfway point in about three minutes. I would have been gloating had I not been so focused on getting there. I swerve hard to the left, passing a box truck by a few inches causing my partner to reflexively grasp for the handle above the door. Apparently, that was what it took to break his silence.

"Slow down damn it! We can't help anyone if we're in a wreck too!" His glare is enough to make me feel properly admonished. Easing the pressure off the gas pedal, I look in the rearview mirror just to make sure I hadn't run the truck off the road.

My eyes move up quickly and then back out the windshield. The glance was quick, but it had been enough. My entire body breaks out in goosebumps as my mind rejects what I had seen. The woman, the one I had just dropped off at the hospital, her vacant eyes staring at me from the rear cabin.

A battle raged within me as I tried to convince myself that I hadn't seen anything. After all, it was impossible for her to be there.

It's just my imagination making me see things. She isn't really there.

Every rational part of me tried to accept that thought, but I couldn't bring myself to take another look in the mirror. To see those dead eyes looking back at me would only make matters worse. A drop of sweat trails a cold line down my neck and between my shoulder blades as I force my eyes to stare straight ahead, nowhere near the mirror.

I was only a mile away from our destination, but it might as well be a thousand. Even though we had the right of way and people could hear us coming for miles, it seemed that there was always a car or pedestrian slowing our progress and most importantly keeping me inside with *her.*

As we approached the wreck the traffic became near impassible. Cars were packed bumper to bumper and thus we were forced to edge along the shoulder. Out of habit I glanced in the mirror before I could stop myself. The space was devoid of dead-eyed woman. All that the reflection showed was the stretcher and the various compartments holding all the lifesaving equipment.

Stressful as the traffic was, I felt myself relax. We were *alone,* she was just an illusion brought on by a stressed-out mind. We pulled alongside the wreck, and I turned around to reach for my EMS pack and froze when I found myself face to face with the woman. No longer was she just an image in the mirror, something I could dismiss without accepting the possibility in which I had gone insane.

I lunge backwards as hard as I can. Pain flares in my lower back as it crashes against the steering wheel. In my panic I don't know where it comes from, and I flail about thinking the thing in front of me has somehow done this to me. A wave of panic fueled by the pain crashes over me, and I flail for the door handle, desperate to escape at this point. Distance, that is what I need more than anything. Finally, my hand scrapes over what I hope is my salvation and I pull. A satisfying pop comes from behind me and the rush of the cool night air.

I do my best impression of an Olympic gymnast and vault out of the ambulance. For anyone who might have seen me it might have looked comical, fortunately everyone seemed focused on the accident rather than the EMT flopping out of the driver's side door.

Once outside, I had a job to do, and routine took over. The person we were there to transport had a severe facial laceration and was losing a great deal of blood. Some of the other responding units had stemmed the worst of the blood flow and now we just had to get her to the hospital to close the gash.

There were two awkward moments while we were there, first, my partner didn't know what to make of me showing up without my pack and two, when I hesitated then took a long look inside when we were loading the victim into the back. I was looking for the woman, but I wasn't about to admit that.

My partner drove on the way back. The idea of staying in the back where I had seen her wasn't high on my list of things I wanted to do, but I was better at dealing with cuts than he was, and we both knew it. Fortunately, she didn't make a return appearance.

When we got back to the hospital and turned the lady over to the doctors, I went in to ask about the woman. I found out that she had died right around the time I had first seen her.

19 LEADING THE WAY

For almost a mile we had been able to see the brIght orange glow that signaled our eventual destination. It was a three-story apartment complex, somewhere one the second floor a fire had broken out. Early reports were coming in that people were trapped by the blaze. Now, as I stared up at the building, it seemed inevitable we probably couldn't save everyone.

As I took my initial assessment of the

scene, I saw that the heat had blown out many of the windows on the second floor. Pump trucks who had arrived before us were already engaged in battling the inferno with powerful jets of water streaming from fat hoses. Tongues of flame leapt out many of the vacant frames, their fiery touch leaving behind black scars on the siding.

Even from the distance I sat, the heat found its way through the layers of my suit. Those parts of me that weren't protected already had sweat beading up on my skin in a useless attempt to cool me. If those other trucks couldn't get the fire under control, none of us were going to be able to face the extreme temperatures inside, and the residents would be sacrificed to the flames.

I took all of this in a matter of seconds. Instinctively I grabbed my helmet and jumped from the passenger seat, ready to go to work. Our Captain had already disembarked and sought out the person who had taken charge of the units battling the blaze.

A little ways away, I saw him talking with another person who was pointing towards the building. With the hoses already manned, it looked like we were going to be the search and rescue team entering the building. In the best situations this job can be dangerous, if not fatal. Going in while parts of the building are still on fire only multiplies the potential problems.

I hoisted the oxygen tank onto my back, and I grabbed the oxygen mask. One of my teammates mirrored my movements, as he also prepared to enter the inferno. The weight of the tank, although heavy, was familiar in its position. I'd trained with this piece of equipment so many times it had nearly become a part of me.

I thought that it was hot when we arrived, standing in front of the building I took an involuntary step back. Even though the fire was limited to the top two floors, the heat seemed capable of reaching down into my lungs and stealing the oxygen within them.

I secured my mask over my face, it smelled of rubber and disinfectant, the oxygen flow allowed me to take breathe freely and cooled my singed windpipe. I took a few deep breaths and met my partner's gaze. We both nodded at each other and pressed forward into the building.

Every floor contained four units allowing us the possibility to clear the first floor quickly. Fortunately for us, the tenants had left their doors unlocked in their rush to flee the flames. We made a quick search of every room. Not finding anyone we made our way to the staircase.

When I opened the door, I didn't know what to expect. If it was completely engulfed in flames, that would mean finding another means of rescue. That would take even more time, and I was sure that was a commodity we were in short supply of.

Luck was on our side in this instance, a light haze filled the staircase and it still appeared structurally sound. We quickly moved up and entered the second-floor corridor. The smoke was thicker, and fire lined the right side of the hallway. Until we could get a hose crew inside, the risk was too great.

Out of nowhere, both of us see a young girl, maybe seven years old, dart between the two of us. She was wearing a dress; it was white with little purple flowers on it. Caught by surprise I didn't have time to reach out and grab her before she ran past us and straight through a wall of fire then disappearing through one of the cut off apartments.

Neither one of us moved for a few seconds, completely dumbfounded by what we'd just seen. I mean, she just ran *through* fire with no protection whatsoever. The prospect of letting the little girl burn to death was just too much for me to handle. Before I could talk myself out of it, I ran forward, following the same path.

I could feel my skin burning for a few seconds even through my protective suit. Oddly, the door to the apartment was shut, forcing me to put my shoulder into it. The fire had weakened the frame and I easily plowed through it and into the fire-filled room.

The little girl stood in a hallway, seemingly oblivious to the heat and smoke. She whirled around and raced down the hallway out of sight. I gave pursuit, the fire seemed to cover the ceiling of the entire apartment. I ducked down, trying to keep myself from being engulfed as well.

When I rounded the corner, I could see a door that had been left slightly ajar. I knew there wasn't much time left before this place became completely impassable. I darted forward, skipping every other door. When I entered the room I see a man, lying on his stomach, not moving. The girl though was noticeably absent.

I hoisted the man onto my shoulder and began to carry him towards the entrance. I knew he would suffer burns on his back, but that was a small price to pay if his life could be saved.

At this juncture, my partner had entered joined me inside. I told him that I still hadn't gotten the girl, but I needed to get the guy I was carrying down to an ambulance. He nodded his understanding and moved passed me to check the other two doors.

I made my way through the building and back outside. By the time I turned the victim over to a paramedic my back was sore, and I was desperate for a breath of the cool night air.

I stood there, trying to force myself to breathe normally as I waited for my partner to return with the child. Five minutes passed, far longer than it should have taken for him to check a couple rooms, and I was starting to worry that something happened to him. I was about ready to go back in when I saw him lumber out of the building, but the little girl wasn't with him.

His gaze found me in the crowd, and he shook his head. I was sure he was telling me she hadn't survived. If that were the case though, he would have brought her with him. There was no way he would have left her in there, dead or alive.

He walked over to me and pulled off his own oxygen mask. "I couldn't find her. I checked every room, even the one you found the guy in, but she just wasn't there."

I'd worked with this guy for a number of years, long enough to know he wasn't someone to miss something like this. I *know* we had both seen her go into the apartment, and I *know* she had run down that hallway.

We spent the next three hours fighting the blaze, but we never were able to get onto the second floor again. When we tried to go back, the fire had spread to the point where the staircase had been completely blocked by the fire. In all, six people died that night in the fire. However, no remains of a young girl were found, and nobody claimed to have a child matching the age or description in their home at the time of the fire.

If my partner hadn't seen the same thing, I would have thought I'd imagined the whole thing. Somehow though, I was led to the exact right place to save a man's life.

20 ON TRACK

The two tablets I had taken over an hour before had done nothing to quell the headache that gripped me since the start of my shift. Every time the siren on top of our cruiser peaked it sent a sharp stab of pain deep into my skull. In a desperate attempt I rub my temples, hoping to relieve some of the pain. So far it had done nothing but give me something else to focus on.

My partner looked over at me, a look of sympathy on her face. "Still got a headache huh?"

The pain momentarily got the better of me. "Wow, they are going to have to promote you to detective with those skill." I cringe knowing Hannah was just trying to be nice. "Sorry, it's really bad right now."

She'd been my partner for quite a while, and it would take a lot more from me than pain-induced remark to turn her mood sour. She smiles at me from behind the wheel and picks up the radio. "This is Unit 57, we're about a minute out."

The radio traffic brought me out of my pity party and reminded me that we should be preparing mentally to deal with the scene we are in route to. A teenage girl narrowly escaped being run over by a train. At the last second an employee at the yard had pushed her out of the way. Unfortunately, he hadn't been so lucky.

One life sacrificed for the mistake of another...

Up ahead I can see the engines, the large steel beasts that drag tons upon tons of cargo across this country. They are still tonight. Usually, they would be lit by the light of the moon, that night thought they are glowing red and blue. The colors of tragedy.

At least fifteen other vehicles were their ambulances, a firetruck, a couple pickups that belonged to the train company and a few other police cruisers. You'd have thought the whole city was out to mourn the death of this tragic hero.

The two of us moved quickly even though it was evident there wasn't much for us to do. It just felt wrong to look as if we were just there to check out the excitement.

The commanding officer on the scene was easy to spot. We made our way over to him so we could get our instructions. Us and a few other officers were told to spread ourselves out in different locations around the train so that nobody would accidentally walk into the scene. Mainly we were supposed to keep the other employees away, but you never know when some interested party might try and sneak a peek.

I was dispatched to a location up near the engine. On my way there I happened to walk by a couple of the train yard employees that were talking about the guy who had been hit. Apparently, his name had been Eric and he'd only been working there for a few months. I had to wonder not for the first-time what kind of person would willingly push himself in front of a moving train to save the life of a perfect stranger. Sure, it was my job to protect people, that kind of thing is expected of you as an officer. But even those of us who wear the badge wonder if they have what it takes when that time comes.

I got to my post and radioed that I had arrived. In the past few minutes other officers had done the same, including Hannah. Usually, things like this are fairly uneventful. Mostly it is just trying to keep yourself alert when nothing happens. In this case though it only took me a few minutes before I noticed someone standing off in the weeds staring at the train. The guy was wearing a bright yellow vest like the rest of the yard workers but something about the way he was looking at the train was odd. It wasn't so much that he was looking *at* the train, but rather *through* it as if it wasn't even there.

I walked over to him so I could make sure he was okay. Someone being in shock after an incident such as this isn't unheard of.

I made sure I made noise walking over to him so as not to startle him. The rocks crunching under my feet would have been enough for most people but just in case I called out to him. "Hey, are you okay? Do you need some help?"

He continued to maintain is thousand-yard stare as if he hadn't heard me. "Sir, I'm a police officer, I'm going to get you some help. Can you tell me your name?"

At this point I had made my way over to him. Something was definitely wrong with this guy, and I wanted to get him some medical help. I pressed the button on my radio, "This is Officer Jackson, I have a yard employee that is possibly in shock and in need of medical attention."

I look down at the patch on his vest to get his name. "The name on the vest is... it says his name is Eric. Wait, one moment." I already knew that Eric was the name of the employee that had been hit by the train and it took me by surprise. Eric wasn't exactly an uncommon name, but it was a bit eerie just the same.

I turned my back for just a second as I finished calling in the medical request. "Alright Eric, I have someone on the way..." In the few seconds that I had taken my eyes off of him he had vanished.

I looked in every direction, trying to see which direction he had gone but I was alone. The idea that someone could have moved that fast to have disappeared from sight, not to mention that he hadn't made a sound. Somehow, he had managed to move across a bunch of lose rock without alerting me to him. It just didn't seem possible.

I hear crunching behind me, and I turn expecting to see the employee but instead it is a paramedic trotting over to me. He stops next to me and looks around. "So where is this guy?"

I really don't know what to say. I mean he was here only a minute ago and now... We stand there staring at each other, an awkward silence stretches on until it becomes uncomfortable.

Finally I can't take it anymore. "To be

honest with you, I don't know where he went. He was standing here one minute and then he was just gone."

The paramedic at least has the decency not to ask me if I need to talk with someone like I've just had a mental break. Instead, he just turns around and jogs back in the direction he came. I know I'll probably be the topic of conversation later, but I don't really care at that moment. I turn in a complete circle once more trying to catch sight of the missing man. I don't see anyone and decide to return to my post.

The rest of the night go off uneventfully, but the man and his disappearing act won't subside from my mind. On my way back to my cruiser I look for one of the guys in the yellow vests. The name Eric won't let my brain calm down. I have to know what the guy who pushed the girl out of the way looked like.

Finally I find one of them standing alone. It is just as well since I don't really want an audience for what I'm about to ask. "Hey, I have a strange question, do you mind?"

He gives me a questioning look but nods. "What did the guy look like who was hit by the train, Eric?"

His expression darkens a little, but he pulls out his cell phone and scrolls through some pictures before stopping and turning the screen to me. The picture is of about eight men, but one face stands out. One of the guys in the picture is the one I had seen earlier that night. When his finger points out the same guy a chill runs up and down my spine. I don't even hear what he says afterwards. It is all I can do to get back to the car.

21 REGRETS

Weary, I sit on the edge of my bed after taking off my belt after working a double. I felt lucky to have missed the worst of the calls that night, but it also felt like the day had dragged on forever. The bottle of scotch above my refrigerator was calling to me, but the effort of getting up and pouring a couple of fingers was just too much for me. Heck, just the effort of pulling my uniform was going to tax me further than I wanted.

Everything is stiff and aching as I kick off my boots and get out of my shirt and slacks. I remember a time in my early years after the academy where I would still be game to go out with the other officers of my precinct even after a long day such as this. Time has caught up to me. Well, that and the people going to the normal officer dives are far younger than I am. It's hard to find something to talk about when everything they talk about seems to be in a code that I don't understand. No, drinking at home is much better.

I know I should take a shower, but sleep is more important than cleanliness right now. I set my alarm for the next day. Even though I don't want it to, my mind does the quick math telling me just how few hours of shut-eye I'll get before I have to check back in. Silently I curse it for the reminder I didn't ask for. Thankfully it doesn't take more than a minute before sleep pulls me under.

When my consciousness returns, my eyes fight me as I try and open them. It feels almost like someone has glued them shut. Frankly, if that were the case, I wouldn't fight too hard since then I could just go back to sleep. I'm still exhausted, so much so that I almost feel like I haven't slept a wink.

Grumbling, I turn over and blindly search for my phone to see how much longer I have. It feels like I have to peel my eyelids apart, but when I do, the clock tells me it is 2:31 in the morning. I have only been asleep for a little over an hour. I unceremoniously drop my phone back onto the table and pull my blankets up around me a little higher. My room feels colder than usual but leaving the warmth under the covers seems worse than checking the temperature on the thermostat.

A heaviness comes over me that hadn't been there before. I had felt it before many times as a police officer, and it had kept me from harm on several occasions. Something in my gut told me I wasn't alone, that someone was here with me. If that were the case, I didn't want to move too quickly for fear of spooking them until I knew I had to.

Slowly I opened my eyes and took in the dimly lit room. As my eyes passed one corner, I thought I saw someone standing in the corner facing the wall. It almost reminded me of a child that had been put in a timeout, but this was a full-grown man.

I didn't know what kind of threat this person presented, but with the fact they were in my home, I wasn't going to take any chances. My service weapon was lying on top of my dresser just 10 feet away, but lunging for it would possibly set the guy off. I had to make a decision, though, and I was intent on taking control first.

Untangling myself from the bed proved difficult, and the first couple of steps nearly had me sprawling headfirst. Luck was on my side, though, and I maintained my balance. Grabbing hold of my weapon, I drew it and turned, ready to fire at the first sign of motion. He hadn't moved, though. There he was, still facing the corner like a forlorn child.

"Hey buddy, what are you doing here in my house?"

I didn't get any response to my question, so I tried again. "I'm a police officer, do you understand me?" Again, nothing. It was like I was talking to a statue.

I lowered my gun and took one step towards him. The movement seemed to dispel whatever had kept him in place because he began to slowly turn around and face me. Even before turning all the way around, I knew the guy was in trouble. Two bright red stains had spread across his shirt. I've done this long enough to know what they were. The man had been shot.

"Oh god, hey, I'm going to call an

ambulance. You have to get to the hospital." Slowly he shook his head but didn't say anything.

"Well, I can't just sit here and let you die." I made a move towards my phone, which was met by an even more vigorous shake of his head.

"Do you know who shot you?" He nodded. "Can you tell me?"

He raised his hand and pointed right at me. My first thought was that I had missed someone else in the room and spun around, raising my gun in the process. The only thing I saw was a picture that adorned the wall. Turning back around, he stood there, his accusatory finger still pointing right at me. For the first time, I looked at the man standing in my bedroom, taking in his facial features. Then, something in the back of my mind clicked, causing my jaw to drop. I'd seen this man before. He was right; I had shot him almost ten years earlier. But that wasn't the reason for my shock. He had been the first and last person I had ever killed in the line of duty.

A cold sweat covered my entire body, and I began to shake as I tried to figure out how this was possible. I'm dreaming, that has to be it... For nearly a year, I had a reoccurring nightmare where I would see myself shooting him. But with counseling, the dream had stopped, but this was different. The finger he had extended pinned me in place.

I placed the weapon down on my dresser with unsteady hands and stared at the man in front of me. He looked just like he had ten years before, right down to the two gunshot wounds. I kept trying to tell myself this was a dream or a hallucination brought about by exhaustion and stress. *Ghosts don't exist.*

"This isn't real. You're dead. I killed you." His blank face took on a look of sadness, but other than that, he didn't move from where he stood.

"This is a dream right, none of this is real?" He just sat there and continued to stare at me, giving nothing away. The fact that I was expecting a dream to tell me it wasn't real is pretty farfetched, though.

"No! I don't believe it! It's impossible!" I screamed at the apparition.

Without speaking a word or giving me any clue as to why he visited, he turned around and, facing the corner from which he came, seemed to shimmer then disappear.

Afterward, I sat on the edge of my bed, trying to come to terms with what had happened expecting to wake up at any moment. The problem with that thinking, I was already awake.

For years I have tried to figure out the reason for me seeing what I did. I don't believe I hallucinated the entire thing, but a reason for him to be there? Maybe he was trying to get forgiveness or even telling me he understood I was only doing my job. Either way, it is something beyond my understanding. The one thing I do know is my opinion about whether ghosts exist or not has been changed.

There are those of us that can go our entire careers without having to draw our weapon. A lot of that depends on where you are stationed as well as some luck. My past literally came back to haunt me. With any luck, he won't return and has found closure. Those of us who do this job may not all see the ghost of the people whose lives we took, but the memories can haunt us too.

22 INSIDE

I was on my way home after visiting my mother. It was the middle of March and an unseasonably warm night, so the walk was more enjoyable than normal. It was around a quarter to eleven at night, and the streets were pretty empty. It was quiet too, other than the warm breeze blowing down the road. I had only planned to stop by at home long enough to check my mail and change my clothes before heading back out, since I had other plans that night too.

I turned onto Saxton, heading for my building near Jordan. In the distance, I could see some red and blue flashing lights, and as I drew closer towards them, I noticed two police cruisers were parked out in front of my apartment. My place had already been broken into on two separate occasions in the past. The apartment was on the cheaper side of the market, so security wasn't as high-tech as a lot of places, making it a common target for thieves and burglars in the area. I'd already upgraded to a better locking mechanism on my front door, but I supposed even that wasn't completely fool proof in the grand scheme of things.

I began to quicken my pace, already fearing the worst. It was just my luck to have the nice evening dashed by some unfortunate news.

I approached one of the officers, with whom I was familiar, and nervously asked what had happened. Although it was late and dusk had fallen a while ago, the flashing strobe lights from the police vehicles allowed me to see enough of the scene to realise my apartment had been spared this time.

The break-in had happened on the first floor, where nobody currently lived. In front of me, the door to the TV repair shop was gaping open, pieces of shattered glass littering the floor outside.

The officer who I was speaking to asked me how long the shop had been closed, since it was a little grotty looking on the outside, and the windows were caked with dust and cobwebs. I explained that it had been almost two years since the owner - my original landlord - had been admitted to a nursing home and had sadly died. His son had taken over shortly afterwards, but the shop itself hadn't been open for several months. The officer looked uneasy at my explanation and gestured for me to follow him inside the shop. Since it was late, I was the only one around who could really give him any answers, which is why I assumed he wanted to show me around the so-called crime scene.

As expected, the inside of the buildings smelled faintly of damp and there was dust on everything, proving the fact that the place hadn't been open for a while. Other than the musty air and grimy surfaces, the shop was exactly the same as it had been the last time I had visited. There were two sets of footprints in the dust which clearly belonged to the two officers who had first investigated the scene, but other than that, there was no trace of a break-in other than the shattered glass. As far as I could tell, everything that the owner had left behind was still in place, albeit covered in a thick layer of dust. If anyone had been inside, nothing had been disturbed or removed. It all seemed rather odd already, but at that point I didn't know the full story. The officer continued with his questions by asking me if anything seemed out of place or disturbed, to which I told him that everything had been left where it was, as far as I could remember. This seemed to trouble him even more, and I was beginning to wonder if any *crime* had actually taken place. He then asked if I knew of any other entrances to the shop, other than the front door and the two doors at the rear of the property. As far as I was aware, those three doors were the only way in or out of the shop. There was a door directly in the back, leading to the apartment's stairwell, and another door leading from outside to the basement. Other than that, there was no other way of getting in or out. We checked the other two doors, but when the officer shined his flashlight over them, both were chained shut and padlocked, and the chains were festooned with cobwebs, making it clear nobody had disturbed them in a while either.

When I asked the officer what he thought had happened, he gave me such a clueless look that I was almost caught off guard. Instead of answering me outright, he told me to follow him back to the front door, where the break-in had seemingly happened. He pointed to the broken glass with his flashlight and asked me if anything looked wrong.

After a few minutes of scrutinising the scene, I realised why he had been so doubtful and troubled this whole time.

Judging from the direction the glass had been shattered, and the way it lay on the outside of the building, it was clear that the door had been broken from the *inside* of the shop. When I asked for a possible explanation, he couldn't give me one. Nothing about the scene added up, no matter which way we looked at it. Someone had broken *out* of the shop, not *in*.

"I hate these weird ones," he'd told me after securing the scene with tape and heading back to his vehicle. "I never know how to write them up, you know?"

I have to say, I understood what he meant. There was no probable explanation for why the door had been broken from the inside, especially when the other two doors had clearly been locked and had been that way for a long time. The only explainable was that there had been someone already inside the building, but why had they needed to break *out* if they'd gotten inside in the first place? It didn't make sense, and something about the whole situation made me feel uneasy, like there was something strange about the place I was only just discovering. The TV repair shop has been completely cleared out now, and is a vacant lot inside the apartment building, but I still get a weird feeling every time I walk past it, especially when it's dark and the shadows play tricks with your eyes. Sometimes, if I'm not paying full attention, it feels like someone might be standing at the empty window, watching me go by. But perhaps that's all just in my head.

23 JUST A LITTLE HELP

It was late one night, just after 11pm, and I had just finished my shift at the station. The parking lot was empty and quiet, since I'd stayed later than some of the other officers, so I hurried towards my car, bending my head against the wind as it picked up.

As I passed by some of the bushes that edged the parking lot, I thought I glimpsed someone standing there, their silhouette clear against the lights flooding from the building behind me. I turned quickly, my eyes scanning the area, but there was nobody there. I figured I must have been mistaken, but the image was imprinted on my mind, and I could have sworn there had been someone standing right by the shrubbery. Reaching for the flashlight on my belt, I approached the area where I had seen the shadowy figure and shone the light over the ground, searching for any prints. But the soil was dry and didn't hold much in the way of tracks. Beyond the shrubs was an empty field, but there was nobody else in the area as far as I could see, and no evidence anyone had even been there in the first place.

I eventually shrugged it off and headed back to my car, thinking nothing else of it.

A few weeks later, however, I had another experience that reminded me of the figure I'd seen that night. I was working another late shift and I was in the office alone, trying to finish up an incident report. As I was poring over some files at my desk, I felt the air in the room suddenly shift, as though someone had entered, but when I turned to glance back, there was nobody there. I carried on with my work, but a few minutes later I felt a breath on the back of my neck, as though someone had come up behind me and blown against my skin. It wasn't warm, but ice cold, and the shock of it made me leap out of my chair and spin around, scanning the space behind me. The room was still empty. There was nobody else there apart from me, and I hadn't heard any footsteps of someone entering and leaving. None of the windows were open either, so it couldn't have been a breeze. It definitely felt like someone had breathed on me.

I was already on edge at the point, my heart hammering in my chest, but as I turned back around, I heard a voice whisper "Help me" from somewhere close by. It was female, like a young woman's voice, and there was no possible explanation for it. I was certain the windows were shut, and I was alone on the second floor. But I knew what I had heard.

The whole incident spooked me pretty bad, and I ended up leaving the office and going downstairs to where some of the other officers were still working, so that I wouldn't be alone. I didn't mention it to anyone at the time, not wanting to come across as paranoid, so I tried to forget it and continue with my work.

A few days later, however, I still hadn't forgotten the incident, and I ended up confiding in another co-worker of mine. It had been bothering me a lot, keeping me up at night, so I figured she'd either help me debunk my experiences or figure out the truth. To my surprise, she claimed that she'd experienced some strange things around the station during her night shifts too.

And similar to mine, it had begun only a few weeks ago.

She told me that she'd been working a late shift in the office when she thought she'd heard someone walking down the hallway outside, but when she'd checked, there had been nobody there. Another time, she too had seen a shadowy figure who was there one second and gone the next, lingering around the entryway to the police station. Like me, she'd tried not to think too much of it and had brushed it off as simply the result of fatigue. But it was difficult to ignore after confirming we'd both had such similar experiences over the same time frame. There was definitely more to it.

Figuring there was some kind of connection between what we'd seen, the two of us decided to look into recent deaths that had occurred in the local area, wondering if there might be a more paranormal explanation for the events. I'd never given much stock to the existence of ghosts, but at this point, I was beginning to convince myself that there was no other explanation for it. I already knew it wasn't just in my head since there was someone else who could corroborate having the same experiences, and for me, that counted for a lot.

After glancing back over the incident reports for the last few weeks, my co-worker finally pulled out a case that seemed to be a good contender. The only death that had occurred in the last three weeks in the local area was a deadly crash that happened only a few streets away from the station, two and a half weeks prior. A woman had been hit by a drunk driver late one evening, while she was heading home from work. The driver had managed to get away with only minimal scratches, but the woman had been pinned inside her car for almost two hours, suffering blood loss and excruciating pain from her injuries. By the time the paramedics arrived on the scene to extract her, she'd already passed away.

It had been a tragic death, and both my co-worker and I believed this woman was the one who we had seen and heard on several occasions. Maybe she was still hanging around the police station, looking for help after the accident. For all we knew, she might not even realise she was dead, and her connections to the area were keeping her trapped here.

24 WITHIN THE TREES

Click, click, click

The turn signal continued to flash on the dashboard as I waited at the light for it to turn green. The fact that I was waiting seemed almost foolish. I was sitting there even though not a single car could be seen coming in any direction. Heck, all I'd have to do is flip on the flashers and I could take the left-hand turn, but in all my years of patrol, I'd never used my job for a way to get anywhere quicker. So, there I waited.

Besides, i wasn't in any hurry to get to the next turn on my designated route. Call me superstitious, but I'd never liked driving next to the cemetery, this route especially. There were older stones that had their names nearly worn clean due to age and weather. Once those names were gone, I always wondered if there was anyone left who would remember they even existed or would theirs be a life wiped away by the sands of time.

The red light finally turned to green, and I made my turn. I could already see the lightless stretch ahead of me that was the tell-tale start of the cemetery fence. Even knowing it was coming didn't stop the shudder that passed down my spine.

It's just a coincidence. It has nothing to do with what's up ahead. I wished that was actually the case.

If it were up to me, I would completely avoid this place, especially at night. But this cemetery had been known to be the location of various illegal activities, (e.g., drugs, drinking, vandalism, etc.), so the three times a night I made my patrol by it was important.

The lights lining the opposite side of the street did little to penetrate the gloom beyond the rot iron fence. I could only make out the first ten to twenty feet, most of which was taken up by a row of maple trees that was supposed to make a person's final resting place more peaceful for the mourners.

I slightly lifted my foot off the gas, and peered into the darkness, hoping to see the same nothing most nights brought. Unfortunately, that wasn't in the cards tonight. Just past halfway I see a shadow moving just behind the trees.

I pull over to the curb and turn my spotlight in their direction hoping to scare them off instead of having to *go* inside. The beam cuts through the night and frames the trespasser. The microphone in my hand freezes halfway up to my mouth as I prepared to tell them to leave.

A black human-shaped figure appeared to be making its way behind the trees. From the distance I was from them I would have been able to clearly make out their features, face included. Instead, all I saw was what appeared to be a black haze. "It" took a few more steps then appeared to turn its head towards me. For a moment we sat there looking at one another before it turned away and walked behind another tree and not reappearing on the other side.

It took me a few seconds to recover my wits. I switched over to the radio and called another unit for backup. In the few minutes that it took for someone to show up I tried to figure out what I was going to say that wouldn't make me sound like I'd lost it. In the end I decided that it made the most sense to tell them I was looking for a trespasser.

As the two of us made our way towards where I had seen the shadow figure, I began looking along the ground for tracks. It was spring and the ground was covered in drops of dew. Every step one of us took left a clear footprint, if someone really was back here, they would do the same.

We arrived at the place behind the trees where I had seen the figure walking and we began looking around, searching for the footprints that would give away the direction they went. Withing a couple of minutes though, the only tracks were the ones we were making ourselves. Whatever I'd seen hadn't left any footprints.

When we got back to our cars, I expected him to give me a hard time about calling him out for nothing. Instead, though he told me that similar things had happened to him when he'd driven by this area too, strange lights, unexplained noises, even seeing figures similar to the one I'd described. Although it did feel good to be believed, the fact that my fears were being confirmed, I'd rather have been called a liar.

25 THE VACANT HOUSE

I was on duty one night, working at the police station's front desk when a call came through from an elderly woman. The line took a moment to stabilize, and at first, all I could hear were short, ragged gasps coming through the speaker. After a couple of seconds, a woman's voice came through. It had the same low, wheezy quality as the breathing, and it was clear she was struggling to speak.

She asked me if I had the number for the local doctor, each word coming out with a painful gasp. It was clear this woman was in pain. I asked if she needed an ambulance, but she refused, simply requesting the doctor's number again. Not wanting to upset her, I agreed to give her the number. I didn't have it on hand, so I told her to hold on for just a moment and put the phone down while I looked it up on my computer.

When I picked up the phone again, barely half a minute later, the line was still open, but I could no longer hear anyone on the other side. The line was completely silent. "Hello? Ma'am, are you still there?" I said, straining my ears to pick out any noises from the other side. I could no longer hear her breathing. When I received no reply, I began to fear the worst. "Ma'am, if you're there, please say something. Make any sort of noise so that I know you're okay," I continued, my voice steadily rising in the hope she would hear me, even if she had somehow dropped the phone.

I heard nothing but the soft crackle and hiss of the line.

I switched to another line and hastily put a call through to the control room, requesting a trace on the woman's number. If she had collapsed – which I was convinced she had – then she would need emergency medical help, and at the moment, I was the only one who could get it to her.

The control room team got back to me quickly with an address for the landline number, and I forwarded it to the closest police and ambulance vehicles. In the meantime, I switched back to the ongoing call with the woman, trying once again to reach her. "Ma'am? Can you hear me? There's help on the way. If you can hear me, please try to respond."

The silence was heavy on the other side, but I was still reluctant to hang up the call just in case she recovered consciousness and needed someone to calm her down. I listened out for even the smallest sound, almost holding my breath, but the whole time there was nothing beyond that dreadful silence.

I stayed on the line until the police arrived at the house. In the distance, I could hear someone banging on the door and then the voices of the police announcing their presence. At that point, I figured it was okay to hang up since the ambulance and police crew had reached the woman. There was no longer anything I could do on my end but wait and hope the ambulance had got there in time to help her.

It was only afterward that I learned what had happened after I'd hung up.

When the police entered the house, they found no immediate sign of the woman. They called out to her, but like me, received no reply.

They found the landline off the hook on the living room table, but there was no sign of whoever had placed the call. One of the officers remarked that the place seemed oddly untouched, as though nobody had lived there for some time, given the amount of dust on the surfaces and the general smell of mildew lingering about the place.

The police continued to do a full sweep of the house, checking every single room and calling out for a response, but they quickly concluded there was nobody there. The house had been completely vacant upon their arrival.

It was only a short while later, when the ambulance turned up, that one of the crew informed the police they recognized the house. They had been called out to it three weeks prior after a woman had complained of chest pains and difficulty breathing. The sole occupant of the house – an elderly woman who had been widowed for a few years – had died of a heart attack in her own living room. By the time the ambulance had reached her, it had been too late to do anything.

Hearing that sent a chill straight down my spine. I felt suddenly dizzy as I recalled the woman's voice on the line, asking for the doctor's number. Why hadn't she asked for an ambulance straight away?

But if there was nobody at the house, or ever had been, then who had put in that call? It hadn't been fake since the control room team had traced it directly to the landline of the woman's residence. Plus I still vividly recalled the shuddering gasps as the woman struggled to breathe while she was speaking to me. It was just like the heart attack victim, who had died three weeks earlier in the exact same house.

The similarities were unnerving, yet the thought I was entertaining was impossible. It couldn't have been the same person. Not when the woman had already passed away, and the house should have been empty.

I dreaded to consider the possibility that what I had witnessed was something paranormal. But even now, I can't shake away the feeling that the woman who had called me really hadn't been at the house. That the whole time, the house *had* been empty, and that what I had heard was some kind of phantom echo of a woman at the end of her life.

26 BEHIND

While this is not my story, I know the area well, and I know the man who told me this story even better.

We work in a big county with one of the top school districts in the state and a new nuclear plant that provides many of the residents with employment. Most of the acreage is farms, but it is starting to have some heavily residential areas as well. It has also made our once primarily farming county into a more populated and semi-rural area. New neighborhoods have popped up all over the place. One old stretch of road had a row of new construction on one side, complete with streetlights and manicured lawns. On the opposite side of the road were nothing but fields of corn and woods. The streetlights tended to be closer to the houses than the road; that is to say, the road itself was pretty darkened, but their glow could sometimes play tricks on your eyes.

    A few years ago, one of the traffic guys in my agency was working the night shift, and this car drove by him as he was parked in the empty gravel lot at the beginning of the new constructions. It had been where they used to park the heavy equipment when they were done for the day as they were working on building the neighborhood. The swerving car was an old, beat-up four-door Buick that did a hard swerve off the road and back on it again before evidently noticing the police cruiser and then sped off. The officer who witnessed the incident called it in as a possible DUI suspect and then proceeded to begin pursuit.

    As soon as that old Buick saw that he was being followed, it took off. At the time, the officer had not yet flipped on his lights or his sirens.

It was early in the morning, most of the neighborhood was still asleep. In an attempt to be respectful of the otherwise empty and quiet area – it was about 3:00 am – the officer chose not to draw attention to the chase and continued to pursue the suspected drunken driver in silence. At this point, the suspect was approximately three to four hundred yards ahead of the officer; both vehicles were traveling at about 80 miles an hour.

      The officer had remained in contact with dispatch for the entirety of the situation. Not only is this standard procedure, but the officer was particularly concerned about the dangers of driving at such reckless speeds in the dark. If a deer, raccoon or opossum, or any other animal ran out in front of either of them, at these increasing speeds, one or both of them could lose control of their vehicles and crash, causing more damage and harm than was necessary.

Without warning, the sedan slammed on their brakes, swerved hard onto the shoulder, and then back onto the road again before speeding off once again as if they were suddenly startled by something. The chase lasted another three minutes as they were forced farther and farther into the more rural area of the county. No doubt the sedan thought he could escape into the maze of gravel roads that cut all throughout the county. However, hitting a gravel road well over the posted recommendation is a sure-fire way to lose control of your vehicle, and that is exactly what happened. The sedan hit the gravel going about sixty-five, lost control, fishtailing as he slammed on his brakes, and went nose-first into a shallow ditch.

The driver was not hurt, and aside from the bumper he was missing, neither was his car. Or that was the prevailing opinion anyway, as the car looked like it had been refurbished from the scrap yard before it wound up in the ditch. It was quite the miracle that the officer and the driver had come to the end of the pursuit with no harm done. By then, more officers had arrived on the scene, along with a tow truck to get the suspect's car out of the ditch.

"Where is my bumper?" he shouted, over and over. "I had one when I left the bar! Where did it go?!" His whole car was beat to hell. In hindsight, the fact this thing had a bumper at all was shocking. To see the man so upset over losing it was even more so. Nonetheless, it fell to the agency to find the lost bumper. It was not at the scene where the man had lost control of his car. As the morning sun rose, the search became easier, but still, no bumper had been found.

The officer did not recall if the car had had a bumper when he began pursuit or not, despite the adamancy of the suspect. At this point, the suspect was in the local jail to sober up. He was being charged with DUI, naturally, but he needed to be sober before any more information was taken from him or given to him. The officer who had run the pursuit and made the official arrest was off duty, but he assured everyone he would find that bumper.

The next evening, the officer came in an hour before his shift was supposed to start with the intent of reviewing his dashcam footage. At the very least, he could verify if the beat-up car in question had a bumper or not. "What do you think, bumper or no bumper?" he asked me as I sat next to him. My job is to handle all the "tech stuff" in the office.

"My bet is on no bumper. That car was so beat-up, it's a wonder it didn't fall apart as soon as it got over 40 miles an hour." I had said.

"Then my bet is on it had a bumper. Which means if it does, you owe me a coffee and a donut. And not from the breakroom." He was ready to start the video.

"Fine. But if I win, then you owe me lunch from the burger joint up the road. You guys keep me so busy I never have time to run up there on my break." I was the only tech guy at the time.

"You've got a deal." He hit the play button, and together we watched what started out as an empty road. A utility truck drove by, followed by a tractor with its lights on. I fast-forwarded through another thirty minutes of video before we saw the sedan in question come into frame. Shortly after coming into frame, it could be seen swerving on and off the road.

"Dispatch, this is Officer - - -. I've got a possible DUI, and I'm starting pursuit. No lights or sirens."

"Officer - - -, this is Dispatch. Received. Proceed with caution. Keep in contact."

"Roger." On the dashcam, the image could have been clearer, but the bumper was there. It was barely there as it was held on by duct tape that had begun to peel and was flapping against the now missing bumper.

"I'll take my coffee with a shot of espresso and some sugar. A simple glazed donut will do." The officer sat back, crossed his arms, and smiled smugly.

"There it is, sure. But where did it go?" Curiosity and the promise to find the bumper brought our attention back to the screen and knocked the smug grin right off the officer's face.

Officer - - - stayed well back from the sedan throughout the pursuit. This gave a wide field of vision; the road, the faint glow of the streetlights to the left, and the complete darkness to the right of the road were all visible. The video continued for another minute and a half before we saw the sedan's bumper fall to the road and tumble erratically to a stop. Something moved across the screen in the blink of an eye and was gone. Both cars sped past the point where the bumper should be. "Did you see that?" I asked.

"Did you see it, too? What did we see? Can you back it up? Maybe slow it down?" It became apparent the officer was shaken. The bumper was there, in the middle of the road, and then it wasn't. And yet, at the time, he had seen nothing, and more importantly, he had hit nothing.

"What about last night? Did you not see that happen?" I was already backing up the video and setting the functions in place to watch it in slow motion. He said nothing, but in my peripheral, I could see him shaking his head.

In slow motion, we watched again. The duct tape gave, the bumper dropped to the pavement, and it bounced and rolled, one...two...three times before teetering to a stop. It had barely stopped rocking when a dark figure ran from the glow of the streetlights across the road, grabbed the bumper, and ran into the fields, never pausing, not faltering. "Again." He spoke. For thirty minutes, we watched and re-watched the slow motion.

It did not seem humanly possible for some*one* to run so quickly, so surefootedly, across a dark road, grabbing an awkward, long object from the ground and carry on into a ditch. An animal could have run fast enough, maybe, but it was not grabbing a bumper up and out of the way. Best case scenario, the animal could have knocked it off the road, but the bumper had clearly been picked up and moved. They wore nothing that would give their size or shape away. No reflective clothing. No flashlight, headlamp. Nothing that any of the typical joggers and dog walkers normally wore if they were out at that hour. Two things were blatantly obvious; the officer would have hit the bumper and most likely have lost control of his cruiser, and we had no idea what or who could have moved at the speeds required with such agility in the dark in order to remove said bumper from the road.

All bets forgotten, the officer scooted back in his chair, stood, and said, "I'm going to go check the scene. Look for some footprints and see if that bumper is still there." I nodded and went back to the dashcam video. Maybe with some finagling, I could get it clearer and figure out what this dark figure actually was.

Later, after his shift was over and we were crossing paths, I asked if he had found anything, the bumper, footprints, anything? "Found the bumper. I sent it to the impound with a new roll of duct tape."

"But that's all? Nothing else?" he knew what I was asking, but at this point, we both felt a little crazy. There was something on that video. A video that clearly showed a bumper being held in place with duct tape, and yet, a figure had potentially saved his life by removing debris from this old clunker, and there was no clue as to what it was.

"No footprints. No hoofprints, tracks, nothing." He shook his head and rubbed his forehead. "The bumper was just lying in the ditch. It was filthy and beat to hell, but there were no handprints, smudges, or anything to even remotely suggest it had been picked up by a person." He shook his head again and dragged a hand down his face as he walked away.

I never heard anyone else talking about this night. I imagine the officer didn't want a lot of attention drawn to the mysterious, dark figure in the video. To be honest, we never talk about it either. It did not matter what I did to the video; the figure remained dark, formless, and unidentifiable. I never got answers for myself or for the officer as to what it could have been. Or who it could have been. Of course, it could just be chalked up to one of those witching hours moments or dumb luck.

27 HAUNTED HALLS

Being a serving police officer, I'm usually quite skeptical when it comes to farfetched stories. After a while on the job, it begins to feel like you've seen it all, and there is always an evidence-based explanation. No matter how crazy the scene or story is, there is always a logical course of events. I am of a mind to question everything and keep digging until the answers come to light. To follow the evidence and use doubt to drive my digging. But as this particular experience has happened to me personally twice, I can't discount it as my imagination or being overtired. I can't shield my doubt behind my skepticism because there is no doubt, and the experience, the evidence, it all comes back to me.

I work at a heritage site. It is one of the oldest functional buildings still in use today. History has been made in this place. Several individuals have worked in these halls. Many people have been condemned and even died within these walls. Some believe the ghosts of the past still haunt the building. I'll admit, I doubt this, or rather, I did doubt this even though there was always a part of me that felt I should believe it.

While the original part of the building was built a long time ago, certain parts have been added to the structure over the years. One such addition is a front corridor. Still, while it is new, comparatively speaking, it was built in 1840, only about ten meters away from the oldest part of the building, the Hall. Anytime I can on duty, I actively try to avoid the corridor as best I can. Walking down the heavily wood-panelled corridor, the walls seem to fall in around you, getting closer and tighter the further you go down. To me, it always feels as though someone is watching and waiting for just the right moment to jump out and get me. Saying that out loud makes me feel foolish, given the pride I have in my uncertainty. But it is what it is, and it is the first area of the whole building I felt a heavy presence.

The Hall, being the oldest part of the building, has seen the likes of Charles I and William Wallace (Braveheart) stand trial before execution, along with many others. The history of violence within its walls can be felt, especially when open to the possibility there could linger the ghosts of the past. Again, there was a time when I doubted this. But I can no longer attempt to discredit myself or the stories of others. An over-active imagination, lack of sleep, paranoia, or whatever other reason could be given; I was the one with it. But then it happened. A moment that changed my mind proved that history could survive and erased my doubt and cynical beliefs. At least when it came to the building.

It happened after another long shift, with another one beginning in only seven hours. If I had taken the time to get home, cleaned up, in bed and back up, and to work for the next shift, I would have only gotten about four hours of sleep, at best. It had been a long week, and that was just not going to cut it. The structure has a basement room with folding beds for service officers on occasions like this. It is certainly nothing fancy, but it satisfies the purpose it is designed to fulfil; a place for overtired officers to catch a few extra hours of sleep before another gruelling shift. I had not utilized this area before this night. Of course, I had heard stories. The other officers who had used the room would tell stories and what I assumed to be tall tales. Most of the time, it would be officers who had been on the job for years telling the rookies to be careful down there, sleep with the door open, and all that nonsense.

    I had been given all the same warnings. Veteran officers had told me their stories, and I had listened with a skeptic's ear. I was not going to be scared of the monster under the bed. I grabbed the overnight bag I kept packed in my personal car in case this ever happened and headed back into the building. I was exhausted and ready to crash. I made my way down to the basement level, followed the minimal signage directing me to the makeshift sleeping quarters, and found an empty bed. The rooms are cool, as I had expected they would be since they are in a basement. The bed was narrow, a single pillow lay at the head, and an extra fleece blanket lay folded at the foot. It was evident the term folding bed was just a polite way of saying "large cot" but still, it would do the job. I set my bag on the bed and opened it to pull out the hygiene bag with my spare toothbrush, toothpaste, and razor. A quick trip to the bathroom, and I was back in the room stripping down and changing into the flannel pants and white T-shirt I had in the bag.

      After settling down for the night, I shut the door and turned off the lights. I expected the bed to feel flimsy and to squeak under the weight of my body, but I was worried for nothing. For being little more than a cot, the bed was surprisingly comfortable and quiet. It did not take long for my exhausted body to drift off to sleep. I recall waking up sometime later and feeling a presence in the room with me. At first, I thought nothing of it. I had been dead asleep and tried to explain the feeling as just being unnerved by not being home. A couple of the others had tried to spook me earlier in the day, and I figured I must have dreamed of something that spooked me awake. And then suddenly, in the midst of my rational thinking, I felt this heavy, oppressive *presence* pressing down on my chest, forcing me into the mattress.

    It was like nothing I felt before. I've fallen and had the wind knocked out of me. I have been on the bottom of the dogpile. I have been tackled to the ground by someone twice my size. None of that compared to the pressure I felt forcing me into the mattress. It felt as though I was paralyzed. The force of the presence seemed to permeate into my every fiber, filling me with the weight of its oppression. Fear had seeped into my mind, and I fought to not panic. I just needed to get up and walk around; to leave the room, get some water. But I couldn't. My arms, my legs, every part of my body was out of my control. Terror ripped through me as I realized I had no physical control over my own body. I was being pushed deeper into the thin mattress. The springs began to creak as they were pressed further into themselves. I felt as though the flimsy bed would soon collapse.

It felt like minutes would turn into hours as I lay there in a panic, unable to move, barely able to breathe. In reality, I believe this went on for about thirty seconds before I regained the ability to control my body again. I had never stopped trying to fight against the presence. When it finally lifted, my arms and legs jerked up from the confines of the mattress. I sucked in a gulp of air and shot out of the bed. I immediately put the lights on and opened the door. I went out to wash my face in the bathroom. I tried my best to chalk this up to a nightmare. I went back to my bed, leaving the lights on and the door open, and spent the rest of the night drifting in and out of sleep. When my alarm went off, the whole night seemed surreal. I couldn't, and I wouldn't believe this had happened. I told myself it was just my over-active imagination and the power of suggestion. Nothing more. I got ready for my shift and went on about my job.

Over the next few days, I mentioned my night in the basement to a few colleagues at work who had also used the room. "That room was creepy! I kept the door open all night." One guy said to a few of us as we stood in a line grabbing food to go.

"Did you feel…I can't believe I am even asking this…did you feel a presence down there?" I asked him when no one gave him a hard time for the fear he admitted to having of the room.

"Yes! It was the weirdest feeling. Like I was being watched. And like I was not wanted there." He visibly shook off the memory.

"Was that all? Just the feeling?" I wanted to know if anyone else had had the same experience as I did, with physical contact, not just a feeling.

"Just the feeling. It really creeped me out." Another guy spoke up after this officer answered me.

"I got the feeling. It was intense. The moment I walked in the room, it felt…oppressive? I hate staying down there. I only stay if the lights are on and the door is wide open." He shook his head and ran his hand down his face. He was not proud of this. He was a big man, towering over most of us and built like a gladiator. To be scared of ghosts or a presence seemed childish and immature. But he was not alone, and no one was laughing.

An uncomfortable silence filled the space between us. Finally, one of the most veteran of us said he heard why or who the presence could be. "They say one of the contractors who worked on the building hung himself in one of the basement rooms. They didn't find his body until three days after he had died." He shrugged his shoulders, grabbed his food, and left.

The rest of us continued to compare experiences. I eventually told them what had happened to me. I was unnerved at the fact they believed me. The influence of the presence had obviously affected each and every one of the police officers I served with in this unit. "I'll let you all know what I find out," I assured each of them when I said I was curious if the old veteran officer was right about the hanging. Further research was wanted by all. Unfortunately, I have been unable to confirm if this was the same room the hanging happened. As far as the hanging? The whole building, the grounds, all of it is married to a history of violence. Who can really say for sure if it was the contractor who hung himself or some other poor lost soul who suffered inside the near ancient walls?

  A few weeks later, I had a reason to sleep over once again. Another long week full of long shifts and one more to go with a short window for sleep in between. I was more reluctant to stay this time, but I did not let fear conquer me or my better senses. I was prepared for the worst but hoped nothing would happen. However, when the presence came upon me again, pressing me into the bed once more, I reacted much differently. I was able to maintain a sense of calm and composure. Despite being pressed into the mattress, I managed to say, "I know you are here. I do not want to harm you. I just want to rest before work." Slowly, the presence began to lift off me, freeing my limbs and releasing me of its oppressive weight. Since that second night, when I spoke directly to the presence, I haven't been bothered. I am still wary when sleeping there, but I have started sleeping with the lights off. I still leave the door open, though.

28 SPEEDING

I used to do highway patrol as part of my duties for the sheriff's department. Most of the time, it was sitting around for hours, waiting for something to happen. In my early years, I would work the graveyard shifts.

One night a little after midnight, someone sped past me, going over 85. I turned my lights on and pulled him over. He pulled over to the side pretty easily. He even did this thing where he turned on his interior light and put his hands on the wheel. With the advent of the internet, more people are doing this. Most law enforcement love seeing people do this because it shows clearly where their hands are. I assumed he was just trying to be a goody-two-shoes so he could get out of a speeding ticket.

I typed the license plate into my MDC; that's the computer we use in our patrol cars. Fairly standard information came up for the license plate. I was confident this would be a routine speeding ticket. I had already decided that as long as they didn't throw a tantrum, I'd mark the ticket as only going 75. It would cut the fine in half.

I got out of the car, put a hand on my flashlight and a hand on my gun. Like I always do. My focus was locked on the car, a little 4-door early 2000's car. I remember how plain and smooth the car looked.

A car door closed. It made my skin tighten. It wasn't the car I pulled over. I could clearly see everything going on with that car. I was expecting another car had pulled up behind mine. There wasn't. By the way, don't ever pull up behind a police car. It would have terrified me and made me feel surrounded. One of my biggest fears about pulling someone over is that someone else would pull up behind me and catch me by surprise.

But what actually happened was weirder. The noise came from my passenger side door. It was dark, so I really didn't get a good look at them, but there was a woman in my passenger seat. I took a glance at the car I pulled over. The guy hadn't moved, so I walked back toward my car. The woman was wearing a highway patrol uniform.

I didn't call for backup. Why would I? This was just a simple speeding ticket. She didn't look like anyone I worked with either.

"Hello?" I called out. She moved a little in the shadows. But didn't respond back. My window was open, I liked the fresh air, so I leaned down. It was like I was pulling over my own car.

"What are you doing in my vehicle?" I asked.

"He's got a gun with him," she spoke.

"What? Who?" I asked.

"He's got a gun with him," she said again, "on the seat next to him."

I opened the door. Expecting the light to turn on, and I'd get a good look at the woman. But when it came on, she was gone.

She vanished into thin air. Nothing will make you feel safe after seeing someone disappear like that. It doesn't matter how much training you have or how fast you can pull a sidearm out of its holster.

I was really spooked, but I still had to do my job.

I could still see the man's hands nicely perched on his steering wheel.

"Sir, I'm going to need your license and registration," I spoke.

Standard stuff. The best way to keep a situation calm is to look calm and act calm.

He reached over into his glove compartment and grabbed his paperwork. On the seat next to him was a hoodie, and peeking out under the hoodie was the butt of a gun. Just like the woman had said. When he saw my lights, he probably grabbed the hoodie to hide the gun.

He was still calm. I wanted to get him away from the weapon.

"Sir, we've had a lot of trouble with drunk drivers this time of night. I'm going to have you get out of the car and touch your nose a couple of times for me."

"I haven't been drinking," he said.

"Then this will be quick," I said.

He got out, and I closed the car door for him. I was putting further separation between him and the gun.

"Do you have a concealed carry license for the weapon in your car?" I asked.

He responded with, "What weapon?"

29 THE BARN

I am a State Police Patrolman. I cover a lot of area during my patrols, but it is typically more on the highways than the backroads. Still, I liked to think I was fairly familiar with most of the areas I was assigned to cover. It often happens a case will cross county lines, and paperwork is needed in both places. Usually, I would start out on patrol, and if any paperwork needed to be taken to another county, I would work it into my patrols. In a minimal effort to avoid paperwork, I would also use these days to take the road less travelled; enjoy the scenery, if you will.

I remember it was July 23rd, 2009, and I was on patrol. I was on my way to the Barracks to deliver paperwork. Of course, I took the less-travelled route. While en route, everything flashed on my unit, and my car stalled; this was turning into a long day. Fortunately, I was able to coast and steer the car into an old washed-out driveway off the county road I was traveling on. Coasting into the driveway, I saw an older gentleman walking out by the barn. He looked my way but kept walking and went into the barn. In the moment, I remember thinking it was a little odd that he hadn't even waved or looked startled. He just kept right on about his business.

    By now, I was getting worked up and frustrated with the unit's lack of power. I tried to get it started, but it was done. I tried a few more times, praying to hear anything that could give an indication of what was wrong. Nothing. I wasn't going to solve this mess on my own. Next step contact dispatch.

    After trying to reach dispatch on the radio with no luck, I noticed a high-power pole transmission line adjacent to the property. I knew then my handheld was useless unless I could somehow manage to get far enough away to prevent interference. My patrol unit and all the equipment inside it were next to useless at this point, which only added to my frustration. The next best option was to use the farmer's phone since I couldn't get a cell signal either. Everything at my immediate disposal was down. I needed to establish contact with dispatch.

For the first time since unwillingly arriving at this old farm, I stepped out of the car and looked around. There was an old, white farmhouse at the end of the driveway. The paint looked like it needed a new coat or two but seemed well maintained. There was an ancient-looking wooden rocking chair gently swaying in the evening breeze. I hadn't noticed the old farmer leaving the barn and assumed he must still be inside. The barn was as old as the house and a classic red color. It, too, needed a new coat of paint and was obviously still functional. It smelled of cows and fresh thrown hay.

I headed out towards the barn where the old man had presumably gone inside and got to work. I hollered, "Hello!" listened for a reply, and then opened what turned out to be the door to the milking parlor. I remember thinking, *it seems awfully quiet in here,* before looking around the milking parlor as I stood in the doorway. I didn't see the old man or hear him, so I hollered "Hello!" for the second time but a little louder than before. Still not hearing anything, I decided to head back out and try the house. I thought, *maybe I missed him going inside when I was messing with my phone*. But as I turned around, he was standing behind me!

I'll admit, turning around and about running into a stoic, stern-looking old man startled me a little. I hadn't heard or seen where he came from. I could've sworn he was inside the barn. But to be behind me, he had to have come from outside. At the time, this was not the first thought that came to mind. Honestly, I was glad to have found him and could finally ask to borrow his phone. The man had no expression on his weathered face when he asked, "Are you having car trouble?" His voice was hollow, like life had got the best of him, but he was still here doing his best to live it.

"Yes, sir, I am. Darn thing is dead as a doornail. I can't even use the radio inside it. Would you mind if I used your phone?" I looked into his eyes and spoke to him like I had been raised to do. He had lonely, pale blue eyes and a face that was creased with wrinkles he probably took on too young. He was tall and still looked as strong as an ox. The years had not been kind to him, but he seemed to be making the most of it.

At first, he pointed up to the house, "We can walk up there," and then he looked back at me, "or you can use the one in the milking parlor. Just as long as you won't be but a minute. I'm fixing to start milking." He took a step towards the barn, anxious to get to his milking, but then stopped as if remembering some long-forgotten courtesy. "Do you want some water?"

"Some water would be great, thank you, sir. And the parlor phone will work. I shouldn't be long at all." He nodded, walked around me, and headed back inside the barn. I followed him into the old red barn and back into the milking parlor. There was an old phone mounted on the wall inside the shop next to the door frame and light switch. Seeing me reach for the phone, the old farmer walked back out of the barn.

I dialled the number to dispatch, "Dispatch, this is Officer ---." I went on to describe what had happened to my unit, my location, and that I was going to need a wrecker. As I listened to their response and did some more explaining, the farmer came back and handed me a glass of water. He then walked in the direction of his milking machines. Dispatch quickly let me know they would have a wrecker out to my location in under sixty minutes. "Thank you, Dispatch." I put the old-fashioned phone back on its jack.

Just as I had the phone back on its jack, the farmer came back towards me, wiping his hands on a raggedy blue grease rag. "You aren't the only one with mechanical problems. One of my old milking machine's pump motor needed a fixing." He kept wiping his hands on that old rag. I got the feeling he was trying to wipe away more than just grease.

"Well, I'll be in your way another hour or so. Dispatch says they have a wrecker on the way. Shouldn't be too long. Thank you for letting me borrow your phone." The farmer nodded and pointed towards my unit.

"Why don't you let me help you get that up to the road so they find you?" he said in his hollow voice as he stared off towards the end of his driveway.

"If it isn't in the way, sir, they can just grab it here. I don't want to make more work for you." But the old man was determined. He started walking to my car; I guess he just assumed (correctly) that I would follow him.

"Nay, they never look in the driveway, so we best push it to the road." I shrugged my shoulders and started to protest but then thought this was his way of saying, *your car is in the way, and I want it out of my driveway* and just went along with him. As we walked to the car, we passed an old picnic table that was set up under an ancient shade tree. "You can just leave your glass there, son." I forgot I was even holding it. I drank the last of it and set it on the splintering tabletop. "You get in and steer. I will push you." The old man certainly looked capable of pushing a car, downhill as it were, but I had to protest.

"I can push while you steer." He stood behind the car, both hands on the trunk and eyes facing forward. There would be no changing his mind. I heaved a sigh and walked to the driver's door. I opened it up and looked back to the old, determined farmer, "I'll help get it going and then jump in." He just nodded. The driveway was inclined, ever so slightly, and made the pushing easier as we were pushing downhill. As soon as the car was rolling, I jumped in, closed the door, and focused on steering safely to the bottom of the road. I looked into my rear-view mirror, waved, and saw the old farmer turn back to his barn.

Forty-five minutes later, the wrecker pulled up to where I was parked and sitting inside my cruiser at the edge of the road. Dispatch said under sixty minutes, and they were not wrong. The driver of the wrecker opened his door and got out of his truck at the same time I was getting out of my unit to go meet him. "Hey, man. Thanks for getting here so quick."

The driver looked up at the farm, "We need to hurry with this hook-up and get on out of here." He seemed nervous, anxious, and spooked. It was evident he was not comfortable being here.

"Everything is fine. There is no rush. Let's get it done right, and we can get on back into town." I assured him as I patted his shoulder and steered us both in the direction of his wrecker. He made short work of getting the cruiser hooked up and ready to tow. We hopped into his truck and headed to the barrack's garage. The drive back was a little awkward and silent. He kept looking at me like he couldn't believe I was sitting there and with nothing to say.

Patrol units take a beating. These cars have so much use and mileage under their hoods; it's amazing they last as long as they do.

Seeing one breakdown is nothing spectacular. So, I was shocked to see an audience when we arrived back at the barrack's garage. Everyone was standing around outside looking like they were waiting for bad news after a terrible accident. I stepped out of the wrecker and was immediately bombarded with questions about my "big adventure" and how I was doing. But the question that really caught my attention was the one everyone kept asking, "Did you talk to the old farmer?"

"I did. I wouldn't call him chatty or anything, but he let me use his phone and helped push my car to the end of the road." A completely normal response met with a completely abnormal reaction. Eyes as big as saucers and jaws dropped as they processed what I had just said. By now, my car had been released by the wrecker driver who had come up to join the crowd. Everyone hurried to go look at the patrol car. "What is the big deal?" I asked the wrecker driver since he was standing closest to me. We were the only ones who had not followed the crowd to go gawk at my cruiser.

"You don't know?" He looked at me in disbelief, eyes wide and face a little ashen.

"No, obviously, I don't. What's going on?" I fought to keep the annoyance out of my voice. I wasn't from around here. I knew the roads of the area, not the history or the people.

He let out the breath he'd been holding, "Back in the early 70s sometime, a farmer shot himself in the milking parlor of that old barn. A couple of families tried to start up a dairy farm there, but they didn't last. No one has lived there since the 80s. It's haunted." He looked like he felt sorry for me like he'd given me the worst news a man could hear. I could feel the blood drain from my face.

"No way. I don't believe it." Even I could hear the lack of conviction in my voice. Another officer was standing close by as the wrecker driver told me about the farm.

"Come on, kid. Jump in my patrol car, and we'll take a drive out there." He was a seasoned officer, probably getting close to retirement. Apparently, he was a Paranormal hunter on the side as a hobby. On the drive out to the old farm, I told him everything that had happened.

As we got closer to the old farm, it seemed different. I knew it was the right place. I was just here. But something had changed, and it didn't seem like the same place. As we pulled into the rough driveway, I began to really see the changes, not just feel them. Tree branches had grown down so low they scraped against the patrol car. As we pulled to a stop at the end of the driveway, I was shocked to see the farmhouse and the barn. It was painfully abandoned. Shutters were falling off the house, no paint was left, and the old rocker had fallen in on itself. We got out of the cruiser and walked to the barn. I glanced to the table under the dying shade tree and pointed out the glass I had left there.

Inside the barn, a thick layer of dust blanketed every surface. I walked in through the milk parlor door and went straight for the phone. Fresh fingerprints had smudged the layers of dust. My fingerprints. I picked it up from its cradle and listened for a dial tone I instinctively knew wouldn't sound. The silence coming from the phone shook me to my core. I placed it back where I had found it. "We can go now," I told the officer with me. He looked like a kid in a candy store. He had so many questions and wanted to do so much more looking. But he realized how shook I was, and we went back to the barracks.

Back at the barracks, we found my cruiser had already been repaired. Luckily, it was nothing major. The positive cable had come off the starter. Simple fix. Curiosity got the better of me, and I walked to the back of my car. Two greasy handprints were on the trunk exactly where the old farmer had kept his hands as he pushed it.

This was several years ago now. I don't work that area anymore. But I have driven back to the old farm because I felt I needed to see it again. The house is gone now.

Apparently, the old place was the victim of some arsonist, and it burned to the ground. Even still, being on that land, it gives me the heebie-jeebies.

30 RADAR

It was the time of year when the days are short, the nights are long, and the weather is predictably… unpredictable. I'll never forget how eerily grey and gloomy the whole day had been.

And calm.

Unnervingly calm, not even a breeze was stirring the leafless branches. It was so cold that day; when the air hit your face, it felt like getting slapped with a brick of ice. A nasty, nasty winter day that made it into the state record books. But, as a veteran police officer, I remember the day for reasons aside from the cold.

It was towards the end of my shift; the sun was near to setting, but I only knew that because of the time. It seemed like that whole week; the sun had been hiding and non-existent. The grey sky faded into a deeper grey, and I knew it would soon be fading into an empty darkness. Wherever the sun had gone, it had taken the moon and stars with it. I was thankful my shift was almost done and was praying nothing would happen in this last hour.

But of course, that is not how Murphy's Law operates. I was sitting in my cruiser, alone since my partner was out with the flu, and parked in the local grocery store's front lot. The grocery store had been closed for about an hour like all the other businesses around had been. Most of them had been closing a little early because of the cold that day. The weatherman on TV was claiming a massive snowstorm was coming in and that temperatures would continue to drop. I was definitely looking forward to getting off, getting home, and getting into my nice warm house.

Anyway, I was sitting there thinking about all this when a black hatchback came flying up the road coming from city streets and heading out of town towards the highway. The posted speed limit was just thirty-five; I clocked this guy at almost sixty. I immediately flipped on my lights and sirens and pulled out to pursue the hatchback. He obviously saw or heard me behind him because it did not take long for his taillights to light up as he slowed down and pulled over just before the "Come Back Soon" sign that marks the city's northern limits. I left my lights on but flipped off the sirens and called into dispatch.

"Dispatch, this is Officer ---. I have an 11-95 in progress. Vehicle is a black hatchback, license plate ***-***." A routine traffic stop and the guy stopped quickly after noticing me, I didn't feel any backup would be necessary, but I knew that's what dispatch would be asking.

"Officer ---, do you need backup?" I could hear keys clacking as dispatch used the keyboard in front of them to run a more in-depth check on the license plate number I provided.

"Negative but will update if something changes." I clicked my radio back into place and put my hat on my head and my fleece-lined leather gloves on my hands. I grabbed the door handle and pushed the door open to step into the near arctic temperatures. The cold was shocking and distracting. My face was the only exposed skin, and still, I could feel the cold throughout my body. For the first time all day, a gust of frigid wind blew. It felt as though it was slicing me to pieces. I shivered hard and gripped my door to close it.

I know my passenger door was not open but, I heard a car door that was not the one beneath my hand gently shut somewhere nearby. I double-checked that the driver of the black hatchback had not gotten out of his vehicle; he was still sitting in his car and appeared to be rummaging in his glovebox. I could see in his silhouette that one hand was gripping the top of the steering wheel as he leaned across the consul and was digging in his glovebox. I had not called for backup, but if someone was in the vicinity, they might have come anyway. I turned to check behind my cruiser and saw nothing but empty roads and the glow of streetlights.

    I had almost convinced myself I was hearing things when I noticed a person in the front passenger seat of my cruiser. Suddenly, my full attention was on my passenger seat. With nowhere else to go and the cold really starting to hurt, I slid back into the driver's seat and shut my door. The woman sitting in the seat was an officer, but something was off. I felt like I recognized her, like seeing someone you know you know, their name right on the tip of your tongue, but you just can't place them. Her uniform didn't seem quite right either. As if seeing a strange police officer in my car wasn't strange enough, I was analyzing why her uniform didn't seem right.

She was calm as she sat there, her breathing barely perceptible. Her hair was strawberry blonde, and she had a spattering of freckles across her pale nose. I hadn't been able to say a word at this point and realized I was just staring at her. She finally turned and looked straight into my face with her bottle-green eyes and said, "He has a gun by the seat." She spoke with a startling conviction. She never broke the eye contact she had established with me. Before I could verbally acknowledge her statement or even ask her how she knew for certain the driver had a gun, she began to fade. I sat confused… but still staring as she seemed to repeat herself one last time. *He has a gun by the seat.* And she was gone.

I don't know how much time passed between hearing the phantom car door shut and the female officer vanishing, but the hatchback suddenly came back to my mind. I realized I was staring at my own reflection in the passenger door window; I looked like a ghost. I shook off the encounter with the policewoman. It was not my imagination. She had been there. But I had to follow through with this traffic stop before the hatchback decided he was tired of waiting.

My stomach was in a tight knot as I got out of my vehicle. The female officer's voice still lingered in my mind; I could almost hear her as plainly as if she was walking beside me. I noticed the driver had his hands resting in his lap. The hairs on the back of my neck stood up, and I knew something was off about this seemingly routine traffic stop. Her warning more than heeded, I approached the hatchback's driver side. The window was still up, which did not concern me at first, given the extreme cold. I knocked gently on the glass with the intent of alerting the man to my presence.

He was looking down at his hands as he rested them palm up on his thighs. From his profile, I could see his brow was knit in an expression of deep contemplation. I tried to tap on the window again, this time with my flashlight. Maybe the motion of the light beam would also catch his eye. He took a deep breath and finally put his right hand on the steering wheel as he rolled the window down with his left. "What seems to be the problem, Officer?" he asked in a slightly slurred voice.

I could smell the whiskey as I stood two feet from the window. I wasn't sure if it came from him physically or from one of the open bottles I could see inside his car. "Well, sir, I clocked you going fifty-eight in a thirty-five. Do you have your license and registration?" The cold was biting through my layers, chomping away at my patience as this man took his dear sweet time rummaging through his glovebox. In the back of my mind, I remembered I had already seen him digging in his glovebox this evening. He should have had it out and ready. *He has a gun next to the seat.* Immediately, I began to feel uncomfortable. The knot in my stomach grew near unbearable. Eventually, he handed me what I asked for. "Thank you. You stay right here, and I will be right back with this." He only nodded and hung his head again.

I walked back to my cruiser backward and gave the appearance of looking at his paperwork. I was focused on the driver, though. What was he doing, and where were his hands? For the time being, he was just sitting there, probably staring at his hands. I was grateful for the warmth of my cruiser as I slid into the driver's seat and contacted Dispatch. "Dispatch, this is Officer --- requesting further information for the driver with the 11-95." Once they were ready, I gave them the name and last known address of the man as well as all the other information they asked for from me.

I was nervous to find out this guy had a warrant out for his arrest. Dispatch was sending backup. Anytime an arrest is made, two officers, at the very least, are meant to be present. To fill the wait time, I filled out a ticket for the fifty-five-year-old man in the hatchback. My backup arrived in just a few minutes, lights and sirens off as they approached my location. We did not want to overwhelm him and cause him to do something rash.

When the officer who came as back up got out of his cruiser, I also got out of mine and told him I had a *feeling* this guy had the potential to become hostile. We agreed he would approach the passenger side, and I would continue speaking with the driver. Together we went up to the hatchback. He had rolled his window back up, so I tapped on it gently with my flashlight again. He rolled down the window again. This time it looked as though he was trying to think himself sober and had gotten himself angry. "Sir, I am going to have to ask you to please turn off your vehicle and step out of the car."

He was visibly starting to shake, and his face was beginning to turn red with rage. My backup noticed this at the same time I did, and he drew his weapon as a precautionary measure but kept it pointed towards the ground. "Sir, please step out of your vehicle," I repeated calmly but firmly. His eyes darted to the right towards the other officer and back to his hands. I sensed defeat in him. It was simply too cold to attempt anything other than cooperation. "Open the door. Put your hands on your head and keep them there as you step out of the car, please." He took his sweet time, but he did follow the instructions I gave him. We were able to make the arrest with no incidents.

More backup and a tow truck came. The additional backup took possession of the car and took it to impound. I took the driver, a wanted man, down to the jail and to processing. Once he was officially signed over and out of my responsibility, I clocked out and went home to my nice warm house. The drive home was quiet. The wind had died again. The eerie silence was back. I thought of the policewoman who had sat in the passenger seat of my cruiser earlier that evening. Something about her was familiar, but even after relaxing at home and getting into bed, I still couldn't place her.

The next day the sun had finally made an appearance. It shone brightly in a cloudless sky; old snow was melting and making the earth wet and almost green. A breeze had begun to blow gently, and it felt like life had returned to the area. I had such a sense of relief and peace flood over me as I drove to work that morning. Somewhere in the back of my mind, I knew it could not have simply been the change of weather, but at the time, that is exactly what I thought it was; a sunny mood to match the sunny weather.

The woman who works the desk at the station handed me the paperwork I needed to finish up, sign, and turn in. On top was also a copy of an old case file from a couple of counties over. I shuffled it to the bottom of my paperwork and decided to start with the report regarding the arrest I made last night. Included in the paperwork was an inventory list of all the items found in his car and a diagram of a generic car marking where each item had been found.

My eyes were instantly drawn to a small red circle with the number one written inside of it on the diagram. It was right next to the driver's seat. The corresponding number on the inventory list listed this item as a 9mm pistol that had been loaded with four rounds. My mind began to race as the woman's voice echoed in my memory. *He has a gun next to the seat.* Her warning had potentially saved my life. Aside from the many bottles of alcohol and other beverages in the car, there was not much else of note. I finished the paperwork in relation to the car, signed it, and moved onto the next report.

This was the arresting report that I had started last night. Included with my own words was the warrant for his arrest from a couple of counties over. According to the warrant, he had shot and killed an officer during a routine traffic stop in which he had been pulled over for a busted taillight. My mind was racing as I thought about the cold case I had been reading along with these reports. I quickly grabbed the case from the bottom of the stack of paperwork and flipped it open to the first page.

There she was. The woman, the officer who had been sitting in the passenger seat of my cruiser. It was her picture from the day she must have graduated from the academy. I saw her name and immediately recognized it as the police officer the speeding driver had killed twenty years ago. Justice had never been served, but it would be now. Her murder happened a few counties over. I'll never understand how she wound up in my cruiser or why, but I do know I will never doubt the fact that her solemn warning saved my life.

31 WHEN THE PAST RETURNS

While on duty one night, when I was a young policeman, I was instructed to get to a residence for a 5150. I knew that a 5150 meant someone at the residence was having some sort of psychiatric issue and needed assistance. I quickly turned on the flashing lights and the siren and headed to the residence.

When I arrived, I began quickly walking up the sidewalk when an elderly woman stepped out of the door. She appeared frantic and filled with worry and concern. I asked her who she was, and she stated that she was the owner of the residence. After telling the woman my name, she began to tell me about her son. She stated that he was addicted to drugs and must have just used too much or some bad drug. I could tell she was trying to stay calm, but she was having a difficult time. I had to quickly assess the situation to make sure that she was not the one that needed help.

I took my time to calm her down and gently asked her to tell me again what was happening. She again stated that her son was on some type of drugs and seemed to be seeing things. Nothing she tried was helping to convince him that he was not seeing what he claimed.

She explained to me that each time her son tried to walk into his own room, he could see that there was an old man hanging from the ceiling.

"The man is wearing an old military uniform from World War II."

I went over and sat down with the younger man, and asked him to tell me what was happening. He looked me in the face and said, "I cannot go into my room! There is an old man wearing a World War II uniform that is hanging from my ceiling!" I could tell the man was higher than a kite, but that did not mean he was crazy. I thought quickly how the mother could be correct; it may be a bad drug. I watched him closely and listened to how he was talking. "The guy who actually lives here told me I should not go into the room." I looked quickly at his mom. She shrugged her shoulders and told me, "It is just the two of us who live here. My husband has passed on."

I looked back at the son, who was visibly shaken. I could not help but begin to believe him as he said, "The spirit who lives here told me not to enter my bedroom. He told me that it is his father hanging from the ceiling."

It was at this time that I stood up and walked towards the room. I hesitated before I opened the door, unsure of what I would see when I did open it. As I entered, I slowly looked around the room, at the ceiling, behind the doors, and even in the closet. I did not see what the young man was seeing.

Just then, I heard a voice that scared the crap out of me. I was not expecting to hear anyone as I had entered the room, and since there was no one in the room other than me, I admit I did jump.

The voice I heard belonged to another police officer, a veteran. I relaxed when I realized who was there with me. The Officer told me that when he heard the address over the radio, he knew he had to come.

He had recalled how years ago, when he was just starting his career in Law Enforcement, he had been ordered to go to a call at this same residence.

The Officer asked me to tell him what I knew so far, so I did. "The owner of the home called in for help with her son. He is a drug user, but she is concerned that it was a drug laced with something that should not be there, and he was seeing things." Upon talking to the son, this is what he told me, "I was told by the spirit who lives in the room that I could not enter. The spirit told me that it is his father hanging from the noose."

At this time, both the older Police Officer and I looked around the ceiling again as he put his arm on my shoulder and stated, "When I came on a similar call to this residence many years ago, it was because an elderly gentleman had dressed in his World War II uniform and proceeded to hang himself with a noose from the ceiling. This occurred in the same room here."

I did think that maybe this veteran officer was just giving me a hard time, trying to scare me. But I knew him well enough to know that a poker face was not something he was good at. I looked him in the eyes and opened my mouth to say something, he squeezed my shoulder, and I knew then by the look in his eyes that he was telling me the truth. But how could this be? No one was seeing the old man hanging, no noose, no World War II uniform, nothing!

Having no knowledge of this case from years ago, I could only believe what he said to be the truth. Is it possible that there were spirits in this home? In that room? The past case was certainly a sad one, but had the drugs affected the homeowner's son to the point of turning a memory into an actual event that only he could see? Was there may be some otherworldly presence at work here?

This would be a case to remember throughout his whole career. It was unexplainable to me and left me wondering how I was going to fill out the paperwork and log this into the system. What I can tell you is that I have no idea if there is any type of help that can be given to the son. Maybe he was on drugs due to what he was seeing.

32 A HELPING

As a 911 operator, you can't help but be nervous every time a new call is routed to you. These people are calling you at the worst moments of their lives, desperate for help. At best, you get people the help they need and help save a life in the process. At worst, there is nothing you can do. That helpless feeling is nothing short of excruciating. You take this type of job because you want to help people.

Just after 2:00 am can be one of the busiest times of the night. With us just getting calls about drunk driving accidents and alcohol-fuelled violence. Intoxicated people also have a tendency to make false reports and hang up before we answer the phone. We have to be careful when we decide to send units to these calls because of the limited manpower available to respond to every situation.

It was around 2:45 am when I heard the familiar beep come through my headset, signalling that I had been issued a call. I responded with my typical opening. "911, what is your emergency?"

Initially, I didn't hear a response from the other end of the line. In almost every instance, you can hear breathing or some sort of noise. In this case, there was only silence.

A few seconds go by before our computers bring up the information for the phone number. Most calls we receive are made from cell phones. In these cases, we will get a screen telling us it is a mobile number unless they have called before, and the operator has updated the information. This call was from a landline. The address was for a home that would take at best twenty minutes before anyone could get there, being it was located on the outskirts of the city limits.

Still not having heard any response from the caller, I was concerned that someone might be in trouble, and for whatever reason, they couldn't speak. With most hang-up calls, they will disconnect the phone almost immediately after the call is connected. Although no noise was being directed through the speakers, the timer letting me know the phone was still connected continued to tick away.

I repeated myself in case they didn't hear me. "911, what is your emergency?"

From the other end of the line came a burst of static that was loud enough to hurt my ears. The shock nearly caused me to rip the headset completely off, but before I did, I thought I heard the voice of a woman asking for help. Immediately I leaned forward, ready to take down any information I could so I could relay anything pertinent to the responding officers. I heard a click in my ears. Looking up, I saw that the call timer was blinking, signalling that the call had ended.

Initially, my first instinct was to send officers and an ambulance to the address on the screen. But the more I thought about it, the more questions I had whether or not I was doing the right thing. With the loud noise, it was completely plausible that I had just been confused about hearing the woman's voice asking for help. We are trained that when in doubt, err on the side of caution. With this in mind, I sent a cruiser to check out the location.
After dispatching the unit, I put myself back in the queue so the system would send me another call when my turn came. This particular night was slow when it came to calls

coming in. Another twenty minutes passed before I received another call.

Even before I could start speaking, the sound of somebody weeping filled my ears. There was no question it was a young female on the line with me from the sounds of it. Managing to calm her down takes a few minutes, but I manage to get from her that her mom has collapsed in the living room and wasn't moving. The call was coming in from a local cell phone, but no information came up on the computer. When I asked the girl where she lived, she rattled off an address that seemed oddly familiar to me.

It took only moments before I realized it was the same address for the call that I had just received. I confirmed the address twice just to make sure I hadn't made a mistake, but both times she gave the exact same location. When I asked her if she or her mom had called a little while ago from their house phone, she insisted that this was the first call that had been made. Stranger still, she told me they didn't have a house phone, only cells. I assumed in her panicked state she was confused and thought I was asking if she was calling on the house phone.

I heard a loud knock on the door in the background, and the girl tells me that the police were already there. Quickly they rush the mother to a hospital with signs that she had experienced some sort of cardiac episode. The only thing that made sense to me was that the mother had experienced some chest pains and called in first, thinking that she was in trouble.

Wanting to make sure someone hadn't gotten the wrong address, I brought up the call log for the call that had come before and dialled the number to make sure someone didn't need help. The phone didn't ring; the only thing I got was an automated recording that told me that the number was either disconnected or no longer in service.

This was the point I started to get freaked out. It didn't seem possible that I had received a call from a number that was disconnected that brought up a location for a house minutes before a woman had a heart attack. If that call hadn't been made, there was a good chance help wouldn't have arrived in time. Even when I went back to listen to the call, the static noise came through, but no woman's voice was picked up. To this day, I still have no idea how it happened, but that mother had someone looking out for her that night.

33 THE DITCH

It was late in the spring, and as usual, it was a really wet night. The roads were slick, and there had been a number of accidents reported along the highway that I was assigned to that evening. So far, every incident that I rolled up to someone had been either going too fast for the conditions or had underestimated the amount of time they needed to stop or slow down. No major injuries had occurred, which I was thankful for.

Driving down the road, I noticed someone standing on the shoulder. Not only was this illegal, but given the weather and time, it was incredibly dangerous too. It wouldn't take but a split second for someone to look away, and their car could drift across the line and hit this person. I hadn't seen any vehicles pulled over to the side of the road recently, so it didn't seem likely that the individual had run out of gas or gotten stuck, so I decided to stop and see if they needed help.

I eased over to the side of the highway and got out of my car, shielding my eyes with my hand as I slowly approached the individual. They just seemed to be staring off into the grass that grew up until the paved surface began. When I got close for the first time, I noticed the clothes that he was wearing. He wore a police officer's uniform, but it was too dark to make out what precinct he was from.

I called out to him to let him know I was there, but he didn't even give me a sign that he even heard me. The guy just continued to stare off into the tall grass as he had been doing the entire time I had seen him. Coming right next to him, I turned to look in the direction he was, trying to figure out what had got his attention.

Even in the rain, I noticed two tracks that were cutting a path through the grass and leading away from the road. When I asked him if there was someone down there, he turned his head toward me, and he nodded slowly without saying a single word. The action of my fellow officer was a little creepy, but I was more interested in seeing if someone needed help at the time.

I charged through the grass, water soaking my socks and shoes almost immediately. Every step seemed a little harder as the mud-caked onto the bottoms of my feet. Every time I lifted my feet, more dead grass came with it making it feel like my feet weighed four times what they should have, slowing my progress.

After about seventy feet, the tracks stopped at the edge of a ten-foot-deep ditch. It was what lay at its base that made me freeze mid-step. A white sedan was sitting at the bottom of the embankment; the red taillights cast a red glow throughout the entire area. The front of the car had been crushed in about a foot from the original position when it had slid down the edge and come to a stop. I couldn't tell if there was anyone inside, but I called dispatch on the radio to get an ambulance on its way in case someone was hurt.

I turned around to yell at the officer who had been standing there on the road to come to help me, but he just appeared to be in a state of shock. He didn't even move when I continued to plead for him to join me. Shaking my head, I edged down the side to where the car had come to a rest.

Using the sleeve of my jacket, I wiped the drops of water off the driver's side window and looked in with my flashlight. There strapped into the seat was a young man lying there in the seat. His eyes were closed, and he wasn't moving. I depressed the button on my radio again and told them we had an injury accident, hoping to hurry along the ambulance to the scene. I told them that there was another officer who was on the side of the road along with my cruiser to help them locate the accident site.

The doors were locked on the car, so I tried to talk to the driver, but even yelling didn't seem to get a reaction from him. I was hoping I hadn't arrived too late to get him to help. Even so, I continued to talk as if he could hear me letting him know that I was there and help was on its way. Some part of me just wanted him to know he wasn't alone, that I was there with him.

It took around ten minutes for the paramedics to arrive. Once I heard the sirens getting close, I went to the other side of the car and used my light to break the window. I cleared the opening and reached in to disengage the power locks.

With the doors unlocked, I opened the driver's door so EMS could get to him faster. Even with the rain hitting him, he still didn't come around, and I could see a streak of dried blood trailing down his face where a cut had been opened from the accident.

I helped them load him onto a backboard and secure his head and neck before we lifted him out of the ditch. By then, a number of other cars had arrived to see if any help was needed. They were all congratulating me on finding the car and kept wondering how I had seen it from the road. I told them that I wouldn't have if it wasn't for the officer who had been standing on the edge of the road. I looked around, trying to find the guy who had helped me save this kid's life, but I couldn't find him anywhere.

The paramedics were just finishing loading the guy into the bus, so I ran over and asked if they had seen where he had gone. When she told me that there wasn't anyone standing there when they pulled up, it had just been my car; I was confused. The officer had seemed unable to move from the place he was standing, almost like he had been stuck in place. Where had he gone? It was raining and the middle of the night.

I told one of the other officers on the scene what had happened and asked him if he would be willing to drive one way while I went the other so we could find him and get him to wherever he was going. I mean, he had saved someone; it was the least we could do. He readily agreed, and we took off in opposite directions.

I drove for a full five minutes with no luck finding anyone. All I saw was wet pavement. There was no sign of the missing officer anywhere. I had to assume he went the other direction since there was no way he could have even gotten this far on foot.

When I got back, the officer who had agreed to help was already back. This being the case, I assumed he had found the guy, but when I asked, he just shrugged and said there wasn't any sign of him. Somehow my strange officer had simply vanished.

Later on, I found out that the kid who had been driving the car had, in fact, survived the accident. He had a bad concussion along with some bumps and bruises, but he would make a full recovery.

I later had an opportunity to talk with him after he was out of the hospital. This is where things started to get odd. He told me that his father had been a police officer when he was alive. Given the age of the kid and from the way he was talking, the father was no longer with us. He even showed me a picture of him and his dad together. The blood in my veins turned to ice when I saw his face; it was most definitely the guy that had been standing on the side of the road that night.

He must have seen my reaction because he asked me what was wrong. I didn't know what to tell him. I couldn't even believe what I was thinking. From all accounts, it seemed as if his father's spirit had led me to where his son was so I could save his life. As much as I wanted to tell him this, I decided it would have just sounded crazy, so I kept my mouth shut.

I have never been what you would call a sceptic. I believe in ghosts and the afterlife, really, I always have, but that night was the only time in my life I believe that I have come in contact with it myself. That young man is alive because his father continued to look out for him even after he was gone.

34 MISSING

I remember this story clearly because it was the night of Christmas Eve. Up until that point, I'd mostly dealt with calls from drunks who'd gotten involved in some minor accidents while they were a little too tipsy, but nothing serious. That was, until I answered a 911 call to a lady who was so hysterical and crying so hard she could barely breathe. I told her to calm down, take a breath, and tell me what was wrong. Even in an emergency, it didn't help anyone if the caller was too emotional to speak rationally.

Once she'd calmed enough to speak, she recounted in a shaky voice what had happened.

"My boyfriend and I… we were watching a movie… I fell asleep. When I woke up, he wasn't here."

She paused there, so I thought she'd finished. I found her story a little odd to begin with, so I said to her: "Okay, ma'am, do you know where he may have gone?"

But she wasn't done. She drew in another shaky breath and said, "I found him… in our closet. He hung himself… *with our bed sheets*." She began crying again, so I urged her to take some more deep breaths. It wasn't the first time I'd dealt with someone discovering a suicide victim, but it was no less harrowing.

When she was calm enough again, I began to walk her through the motions of cutting down the body and beginning CPR. She wasn't sure how long she'd been asleep for, or how long her boyfriend had been hanging there, but there was always a chance of resuscitation, no matter how small or unlikely it may seem.

She was still frantic and borderline hysterical as she cut the bedsheets, and I heard the body thud to the ground through the phone. She began crying again while doing the chest compressions. I counted alongside her the whole time, making sure she knew she wasn't alone.

It was about mid-way through the CPR when, through the phone, I heard the woman's boyfriend make a long, raspy exhale. It sounded like something out of a horror movie, that low, gurgling rattle from somewhere deep inside.

The woman grew hysterical again, crying as she called out her boyfriend's name. "Oh my god, he's breathing," she sobbed down the phone. "Please breathe, baby. Please breathe. That's it." But from experience, I knew she was wrong. He wasn't breathing at all. It was the sound of all the excess air leaving his lungs. I knew he was already gone.

When the police and ambulance crew arrived, they found the guy dead, past the point of revival. The woman was hysterical, inconsolable. I felt horrible for her. She'd been so convinced that her boyfriend was breathing again, only to find out he was still dead. That's really the only 911 call that ever really stuck with me as much as it did.

But the story doesn't end there. A few months after the incident, we received another call from the house next door to the address where the man had committed suicide. They reported seeing a man standing on the sidewalk outside, just staring at the house for hours on end, before just fading away. When they were asked to clarify if they meant he walked away, but they were adamant he simply just… disappeared. We sent units over to investigate the area, but, as expected, they found nothing. They ruled it out as nothing of importance and didn't investigate any further.

But if you were to ask me, I think it was the spirit of the man who had hung himself in the closet. Maybe he'd come to say goodbye, or maybe he was just lost and lingering on. But who really knows?

35 BURNT

The entire vehicle shook as we sped through town towards our destination. Already the pillar of black smoke could be seen growing closer in the distance. A twinge of anxiety coursed through my body at the color. It foretold the possibility of injured people and increased danger. White smoke came from natural things burning, as opposed to black, which was from the made substances being devoured by the extreme temperatures of the fire.

Adjusting my helmet, I took a few deep breaths trying to steady myself for the job to come. This is what I had signed up for, what I lived for.

Gravel scaped under the tires as our engine came to a stop. From the first moment, I could tell this was one of the worst possible situations. Even at this distance, I could see fire spitting out of nearly every window from the third and fourth floors. It meant that the people above it were trapped with little means of escape. The ladder trucks just couldn't reach the highest floors, so it was up to us to stop it before that happened.

Our team was a well-oiled machine when we went into action. Every one of us knows what our responsibility is before we even arrive. I grab one end of the hose and run towards the nearest hydrant. My partner and I connect it and start the flow going towards the engine.

From there, things start to move quickly. One of the other firefighters helps me hoist the oxygen tank onto my back as I check the seal of the mask on my face. The whole process takes less than 30 seconds, and I'm ready to enter the building. We all know there isn't a lot of time and before the building isn't going to be safe for us to enter. I grab my rescue axe and charge into the door that is already dripping with water.

The first floor is still clear of smoke, and the clearing of the rooms is quick since all of the residents and offices were quick to react to the alarms. The sweep of the second floor is just as quick as we find room after room abandoned.

Entering the stairwell up to the third floor is like running into a wall of heat. The mask already makes the work hot, and the fire makes it nearly suffocating. Still, I press forward and carefully open the door giving me access to the floor. Everything around me looks like it is on fire; even the cinder block walls are not spared from the extreme heat.

I move to the right and start going

door to door, trying to find any survivors, but before long, it becomes clear we can't go any further without taking careless risks. We radio to the chief, and he tells us to evacuate the building in hopes of us getting control of the blaze with the hoses.

This is the hardest part of the job, leaving people behind. Me and three others look helplessly at the fire, knowing there isn't anything we can do. With a shake of my head, I turn and begin my descent with a heavy heart.

Once outside, we help people escape from windows from the ladder truck but know that there are others who will never leave the building. I do my best to block out the dark thoughts as I concentrate on doing my job.

It takes almost three hours but finally, the blaze is under control. The inferno has gutted four floors of the building. We are now preparing to reenter the building, knowing full well what we're going to find when we get there.

When we reach the fire-damaged area, the work is slow going. Every step is tested with prods to make sure the floor is still able to hold our weight. We sweep every room on the floor and thankfully find that everyone seemed to have gotten out safely.

I was the first person to get onto the fourth floor. Knowing this had been the first floor to be cut off by the fire, it was the likely place where we would start finding people who hadn't made it out. I'd seen death before, including men and women I work with, but I never got used to it. Some people say they had, but not me. I saw everybody as a failure on my part.

I started walking down a hallway looking through doors on both sides. I had made it only a few doors when I began to hear someone coughing from somewhere down at the end of the hallway. Based on the damage in this area, I didn't think it was possible for someone to have survived, but it does happen.

Every part of me wanted to rush down to where I heard them, but I knew that I couldn't do them any good if I was hurt in the process. I forced myself to move slowly, probing every part of the path ahead. I kept telling them to talk to me, to hold on, and that I was on my way.

I had only made it about halfway when I heard a violent hacking sound, and then a scream pierced the air. "Help me! Oh God, please!"

All hesitation was stripped from me, and I recklessly charged forward down the hall, hoping to avoid any serious accident. The door from which I had heard the scream come from was closed, so I tried the handle. Locked.

"Help me..."

The voice was much softer now, weaker. I knew they couldn't have long, so I did what I had to; I took my axe and began swinging with everything I had. Fueled by adrenaline, it only took a few swings to turn the area around the handle to splinter, allowing me to enter the room.

The room was almost completely destroyed. Scorch marks covered nearly every surface. Next to one wall, a figure huddled, their skin blackened from the fire. There was no way this could be the person I was looking for; they had been dead for quite a while. The only other place they could be was in the closet, but when I looked, there wasn't anything in there but office supplies that had been ruined.

I was confused. I swore this had been the room the voice had come from. I had heard someone calling for help. I retreated into the hallway and checked every door around me, but the only person I found was the victim in the first room. It just didn't make any sense.

I radioed in that I had found a body which set off a number of people showing up to photograph and take away the body. The sound of the coughing and voice wouldn't leave my mind. I didn't think I could have heard something else and mistaken it for words, but I didn't know what else to think. I wished someone else had been there so I would at least have someone to back up my story.

When the paramedics arrived, they confirmed my suspicion the victim had been dead long before I had gotten there. It further brought into question everything I thought I heard. Stress can make a person hear and see some strange things, but this had never happened to me before.

The incident had shaken me enough that I needed to talk to someone, but I didn't want to do it over the open channels. I went back down to the ground floor and found my captain coordinating the efforts of the engines as they put out any remaining hotspots in the building. When I told him what had happened, his reaction wasn't what I had expected. He pulled me aside and told me he would talk with me later about it, but he needed me to help finish clearing the building.

A few days after the fire, he called me into his office and told me to shut the door. It is never a good thing when a meeting starts this way, but what choice did I have? I had been worried that he was going to tell mc I had to get a mental evaluation before I could come back since I had been hearing things, but again, he surprised me.

"Do you believe in ghosts?"

The question knocked me on my heels. I stammered for a few seconds before telling him that I thought I did. The answer apparently satisfied him, and he went about telling me of an incident he had early on in his career when something similar happened to him. A disembodied voice coming from a person that was already dead. He told me that a lot of people think that when a person dies in terrible ways, their spirit can stay behind. He attributed both of our experiences to this. I had to admit that being burned alive was one of the worst ways a person could go.

To this day, I still question what really happened in that hallway. Did I hear the spirit of a person calling out for help even after they had died? Was it my imagination? Something else? I don't know the answer to that question. If it was someone's spirit, I might not have been able to save them, but I hope they found peace.

36 NIGHT SCHOOL

You're guaranteed to experience something weird when you're part of the military police. Just ask anyone who's been around a while, and they're sure to know at least one military ghost story. I know from experience that weird things happen at night, especially in areas that have seen a lot of warfare and bloodshed, like old hospitals. Places haunted by death are magnets for unordinary activity.

I was stationed at an old elementary school one year, and this was this area around the back of the building that would always creep me out. Whenever I was walking around there, doing security checks late at night, I'd always get the feeling of being watched. The whole place just made me uncomfortable, and I'd get out of there as soon as I could.

One night, I found one of the side doors to the school hanging open, when it clearly shouldn't be. I radioed for another unit to join me and backed up several feet to a corner, where I could see the door while remaining hidden. It took around twenty to thirty minutes for my backup to finally arrive. During that time, I had my back to a wall and could see down the side of the building to the corner, around 70 or more feet ahead of me. As I was staring straight ahead, I saw a figure appear at the far corner. It didn't come around the wall or anything. It just appeared, almost out of nowhere. The figure was a young female, maybe between 9-12 years old, and was wearing a red jacket or an old-fashioned cloak. It was too dark to make out too many details, but her clothes didn't seem modern.

They looked like the belonged more to a 20s to 50s style of fashion.

It must have been around two in the morning at this point, so I took a step forward and told the child that it was late, and she should be at home. Before I was finished talking, the figure just completely vanished. I sprinted forward to where she'd been standing, checking to see if she'd run around the corner, but the area was completely empty. It was an open space, and I got there in less than ten seconds after she'd disappeared, but she was nowhere to be seen. I went around the whole building with my Surefire but didn't see her or any trace of her anywhere. It was almost as though she hadn't been there to start with, but I was certain of what I'd seen. Even in the dark, it was difficult to imagine such an obviously human figure.

I returned to my position near the side entrance of the school, just as the back-up I'd called arrived. They went in and searched the whole building for any sign of an intruder, but it was all clear. They told me they'd heard a noise in the gym, like the sound of someone bouncing a basketball, but when they'd checked, there was nobody inside. They did find a basketball, though, in the middle of the floor, as though someone had used it recently. Nevertheless, the whole place was empty and the only way in or out was through that open side door, through which I'd seen nobody go in or out apart from the guys.

When I told them what I had seen, the team leader just laughed and said that a lot of stuff like that goes on there at night. Apparently, it's not unusual to see figures wandering around at night, there one minute and gone the next. I never saw that girl again, but the memory still haunts me.

Had I really seen a ghost that night? Or had it been something else?

37 SHADOWED

I was sitting at the bottom of a small hill in my unmarked car, monitoring the traffic on the highway ahead of me. It was around two to three o'clock in the morning, and it was completely dark out. The roads were shrouded in gloom, and the moon was only a thinly veiled crescent in the sky.

Because of the long stretch of road, the whole highway was known for drivers going 15-20mph over the speed limit, so it was a good spot to hide out and flag down law breakers when they were least expecting it. Despite that, most officers at the precinct refused patrolling the area because of some rumours surrounding the same hill I was parked at.

The area had something of a reputation to the locals, due to being a crime scene almost twenty-six years previous. The body of a murder victim was discovered on the hill, but the case was never solved due to lack of evidence and a positive identification of the victim. Hyped up by the local media, no doubt, the area was long suspected of being 'haunted'. People reported feeling nauseous or dizzy when hanging around the hill, and even the officers had bought into it, refusing to be stationed here. I didn't really believe in that kind of thing, so it didn't bother me when I was assigned this spot for traffic monitoring.

As I was sitting there, keeping an eye on the horizon for any oncoming headlights, something drew my attention. A shadow had just passed across the back of my unit, coming round from the passenger side. I blinked a couple of times, clearing the haze from my eyes from staring into the distance for too long, wondering if I was seeing things. But then I saw the shadow cross over to the driver's side, moving across the front of the vehicle.

Other than the pale glimmer of the moon, there were no lights on the highway. The road was shrouded completely in darkness, making it impossible to see if there was anything there that could have cast a shadow.

That's when I heard footsteps too. It was only faint, but it sounded like grass crunching softy beneath someone's shoes, to the left of the vehicle.

I squinted through the window, but I still couldn't see anything beyond the gloom.

Thinking there was somebody outside the car, I started up the ignition and switched on my headlights, casting a dazzling glare across the grass in front of the car.

With the whole area lit up, I looked out of each window to see who was out there. There was nobody. The shadow had been too large to be animal, but there was nowhere out here for a person to hide. The hill was completely empty.

I began to feel somewhat unsettled by the thought there might be someone out there, walking around my car. It must have just been my imagination that conjured those shadows, but somehow, I felt convinced I wasn't alone.

Shaking my head, I flicked off my headlights and settled back in my seat. I kept my hazard lights on, casting an eerie red glow around the car, just in case anything was out there.

The road itself had gone unusually quiet. Although it was the early hours of the morning, there were usually still cars on the highway at this time. Yet I could barely see the glimmer of a high beam in the distance.

The wind began to pick up outside, making the unit rock slightly. The grasses on the hill began to sway, creating anomalies in the shadows.

I forced myself to keep my eyes on the road, watching the horizon. Unease gnawed at my stomach.

Something moved past the car; a shadow, darting across my periphery.

My heart jumped, and I reflexively switched the headlights back on, flooding the hill.

There was nobody out there. No movement but for the wind rustling through the grass.

I decided it was time to leave. There hadn't been a car driving past in some time, and I was starting to spook myself out. There wasn't much point in hanging around anyway, especially since my shift was coming to an end.

As I set the car into motion and drove onto the highway, I flicked a glance up to the rear-view mirror. For a moment, my blood went cold. It looked as though there was someone stood in the shadow of the hill, watching me drive away. I quickly dragged my eyes back to the road, scolding myself for being silly. I was letting those stories get to me, that was all.

I didn't stop feeling uneasy until I reached the next town, where the streets were well-lit and there was more traffic on the road. It was then that something blinked on my dashboard: the security camera. I pulled over to the side of the road and took the camera down from its hook. It must have been recording since I hit my emergency lights, which meant if there had been someone out there on the hill, the camera would have caught it.

I rewound the footage to where it began recording, and hit play, my heart thumping with nervous anticipation.

I hadn't imagined the shadow after all. The video clearly showed a figure walking around the car, starting from the passengers' side of the vehicle before moving around to the drivers' side. Then, for about half a second after, the entire video went black. It was almost as though someone had put their finger over the lens, smudging the visual. After that, it went back to normal, and there was no longer a shadow in view. I wound the tape forward a few more minutes, but the shadowy figure didn't return.

I set down the camera, unease settling in the pit of my stomach as I wondered what it could have been. The shadow had no visual features, nothing to suggest it was a person, but what else could it have been?

I tried not to dwell on it as I drove back to the station. Maybe I just needed some rest, and the whole thing would seem silly in the morning.

Nevertheless, the next time I was asked to go to the hill to monitor traffic, I refused.

38 BENEATH THE FLOOR

The cadaver dog's nose passed back and forth along the ground as we canvassed the area hoping to find the body of our 22-year-old victim. Hoping to give the family closure, we were here to give the family a chance to bury their daughter.

We moved in a slow gird pattern ensuring we covered every square inch of ground outside the house. If we didn't find her here, we would try searching the house again. After that, I didn't know, this was where she was supposed to be, at least that is what {he} had told us in exchange for a few lousy extra privileges.

Every time the dog paused for the briefest of seconds my heart seemed to beat a little faster. I wanted to find her, more than I cared to admit. Tragic as it may be, doing so would give the family a chance to morn her, rather than holding onto the hope, false as it may be, that someday she would show up at their door, safe and sound.

Unfortunately, every pause was met with a quick resumption of the search. If Tango found something he was trained to sit down on top of the suspected area. He was good at his job, and if she was here, he would find her.

It took us almost two hours to make our way around the outside of the home. He hadn't sat down which meant she, in all likelihood, wasn't out here.

Teams had searched the house already, but the captain had wanted us to "give the dog a shot". None of us really expected to find anything in the building but at this point we were starting to get desperate.

From the moment the two of us entered the house Tango started acting strange. He was usually very easy going and easy to control. Now though he was pulling erratically on his leash as if unsure whether he should run to or from something. It was taking everything I had just to keep hold of his leash.

We took turns dragging each other from room to room depending on what his mood was. His snout moves frantically back and forth along the floor, still searching for a scent. We cleared rooms quickly, at this point I was more along for the ride than actually controlling Tango.

I went to open one of the doors to a bedroom to allow him access and stepped forward quickly expecting him to continue with his frantic pace not noticing he had frozen in place. I twist, trying to avoid him, knowing I'm going to fall and hoping I don't crush him.

It's only a couple of inches, but somehow, I manage to circumvent the statue of a dog in front of me. I turn over and stare at Tango, trying to figure out what has gotten into this crazy mutt. One minute he is out of control and the next he sends me sprawling to the floor, unmoving.

I'm about to scold him, but then he surprises me for the second time in less than a minute. The heckles on the back of his neck are standing on end and his teeth are bared. A low growl escapes his throat, a warning. He isn't looking at me though, he is staring straight into the room with a laser focus in his eyes.

I've never seen him like this before. Sure, he is trained to protect himself and me when it is needed. That training though hasn't been needed.

The look in his eyes is frightening, and I'm glad he isn't trained on me.

Still on the ground I look into the room a little afraid of what might be the cause of this odd behavior. The room is empty, bare walls, bare floor. "Tango, what's gotten into you? Is there someone in there?"

I finally stand causing him to look up at me and gives me a pitiful whine before turning back. This time though he starts barking, and nothing I do seems to be able to stop him. I'm about to call someone to help me when he suddenly bolts. I'm not ready and the leash is torn painfully from my hand.

I know I have to go after him but first I want to find out if there is something in here that might have caused the strange reactions. I take one step inside the room, and it feels as if the temperature drops nearly thirty degrees.

I jump back into the hallway, unsure

of what had just happened. Tentatively I stick my hand out, testing to see if it was just my mind playing tricks on me. I can still feel the cold, it's almost like putting my hand over a vent while the air conditioner is on.

Now expecting the temperature change I venture deeper into the room. There was no clue as to what could be causing the anomaly, but I had a job to do. Off to my left a noise draws my attention. It sounds like scratching and it's coming from the direction of the only other door in the room.

It must be a mouse or something...

Slowly, I make my way over to the door and turn the handle, expecting a small creature to scurry out as soon as I open it. No such thing happens, the only thing I see is a few empty hangers and a small, latched opening in the floor, probably the entrance to a crawlspace.

The scratching seems to be coming from beneath the floor. Now it is louder, almost frantic. My handshakes as I reach for the handle, not sure what I'm going to find on the other side. Like a band aid, I grasp the handle and fling it open. Instinctively I jump back trying to gain some distance between me and whatever is down there.

All I can see is a few inches into the opening from the angle I am at. I shuffle closer ready to follow Tango's example at a moment's notice.

It takes me a few false starts before I find the courage to turn on my light and look down in the hole. When I do my breath catches in my throat. The area is a small concrete square, only about eight feet by eight feet. But what is lying in one corner has me my heart beating out of my chest. Curled in a ball at the bottom is some skeletal remains that are obviously human.

I immediately called for help on the

radio. The immediately room becomes a hive of activity as investigators dissect every inch of the space. When asked me how I found the body I told them about the scratching, the thing was though... the only thing down there was the skeleton.

39 SQUATTERS

I could hear the sound of the snow and ice being flattened beneath the tires of my cruiser as I made my way slowly through the city. People were scarce on the streets today. Only the bravest souls were willing to subject themselves to the sting of the mid-December air. Windows were decorated with various Christmas decorations announcing the coming of the holiday which reminded me I still had to pick up a few last-minute gifts for the wife and kids.

I loved being a police officer this time of year. Most of the calls tended to be about two things, homeless people squatting in one of the abandoned buildings trying to stay warm or theft. This could be a hard time for a lot of people, I understood that, but that didn't mean someone could break the law.

Turning a corner I noticed an open door off to the left side of my car. I knew this place hadn't been occupied for quite some time and I was sure that I had seen the door shut earlier in my patrol. Ordinarily the people staying in a place like this were going to be more careful about covering up their tracks. Carefully flipped around and parked right outside.

Walking up on the sidewalk I looked up at the two-story building wondering what it had been in its previous life. No signs or markings gave a clue what purpose it served before now. My eyes made their way down the building and onto the ground. A clean white surface led up to the opening. Although odd, it was entirely possible someone had already been here before the snow started which would explain away the absence of footprints, in that case though leaving the door open allowing the heat to escape made even less sense.

I take a few steps into the building and announce my presence. "This is Officer Morrison. I'm a police officer, is anyone in here?"

For a few seconds nothing happens and then a loud knock comes from somewhere up on the second floor. My eyes look back and forth trying to locate the stairs, but they are hidden somewhere further in.

"Hello?" This time no sound to indicate someone else is here with me.

Slowly I make my way down the

halls trying to find someone. Room by room I find signs that people had been here, but the items are in various states of decay and are covered in dust.

I leave the last room on the first floor when I believe are footsteps rushing across the floor above me. They are not loud and come close together leading me to believe they are that of a child. If that is the case, I'll have to call a shelter that will take them in.

The stairs are at the very back of the building. The wood groans as it flexes under my weight. The light patter of footsteps is still going on but now I start to hear the sound of children, maybe two or three giggling as well.

"My name is Officer Morrison, I'm a police officer. I'm coming up, okay." I say it loud enough that anybody upstairs would have been able to hear me.

I make my way up the last few stairs. When my boot touches the floor of the landing the footsteps and the giggling seem to be swallowed by the silence that follows. The eerie atmosphere causes me to stop in my tracks, thinking I can wait their stillness out.

Seconds go by, then minutes and the only sound that comes is that of my breathing. *These are either the most patient children ever or I'm hearing things.*

The upper floor is laid out just like the one below it and I proceed to go about my search in a similar fashion. I get about half of them cleared when I start to hear the sound of giggling coming from a door up ahead of me.

Finally, I found you.

Expecting to find children on the other side of the door I decide to knock. "I'm a police officer. I'm coming in."

Of all the things I find on the other side, this was the last thing I would have said. One window lay in the wall opposite the door provided the only light inside the otherwise featureless room. I could see a small pile of rubbish that had been moved to one corner of the room, but no kids. I had been positive I had heard signs of life just seconds before and now, nothing.

I looked out the window, checking to see if they had possibly gone out a fire escape in hopes of alluding capture. The problem was, no fire escape was present. I was dumbfounded. With no other doors or means of escape there wasn't anything to explain the empty room.

Walking over to the small pile of garbage I saw a small piece of paper lying on top, so I walked over and picked it up. In crayon, scrawled in a child-like manner was a picture of a police office, his uniform similar to my own.

The sound of a child's giggle coming from behind me caught me by surprise. I spun around, but no one was there. A rush of cold air brushed past me causing the hairs on the back of my neck to stand on end. At this point I was starting to get scared. Something weird was definitely going on in this place.

I rushed from the room and made my way outside, too afraid to look behind me the entire way. I didn't stop until I was inside my cruiser, painting in my seat. That is when I noticed in my hand, I still held the picture of the police officer. I opened the door and threw it outside onto the street as if it was a snake about to bite me.

I looked to the door, which was still open. Shaking my head, I drove off, unwilling to even go back to shut the door. That was someone else's problem now.

40 LIFELESS FLIGHT

My entire body vibrated along with my jump seat as the helicopter powered its way towards the accident site. If that wasn't bad enough, the engine turning the massive roars that were keeping the aircraft aloft made talking to one another without the headset I was wearing impossible.

"We're about fifteen minutes out."

The pilot informed me.

Even without having to rely on roads, the location we were headed made this flight the only chance we had to get the critically injured patient to the hospital in time. Even then, this was likely not going to matter.

A climber had fallen from a height of nearly fifty feet. Details were scarce, but we were told by the dispatcher. "Severe head injury..." was all we knew. What made matters even worse is we would be trying to find a landing zone in a rocky area, plus the sun was just dipping below the horizon reducing visibility and making it more difficult to spot the victim and her friend. Black and whites were on route, but it was likely the injured woman would be dead before they arrived.

I was all keyed up and ready to be there already. I didn't want this to become a DOA. "Come on! Can't this piece of junk go any faster!"

The pilot looked back towards me, I didn't mean for him to hear what I said, but the headset had made him aware of what I was thinking. The look he was giving me told me that he wasn't pleased with my comments on his flying. "We're going as fast as we can."

"Sorry about that." I wasn't really sorry. "I just hate losing people." This was the only true part of the apology.

"It's fine." From his tone I could tell it wasn't fine, but he turned away from me and focused his attention outside the front window.

Whether he actually sped up or not I couldn't tell but the flight seemed to end quicker than I thought it would. Before long we had located the climbers. Two women stood by a prone figure that lay motionless on the ground.

The third climber complicated matters. It was already going to be a tight fit. If the other climber was also injured trying to work around them was going to be difficult. It was likely that we would have to leave the other two women here and take the fall victim with us.

"I thought there was only two people here." I said to myself.

"What's that?" The pilot said.

"Nothing. Just thinking out loud."

We hit the ground with a solid thud, and I flung the door open and ran in the direction I had seen them standing. He had landed the chopper to a flat area about fifty feet away. I had grabbed the backboard, which I put on the ground next to the woman ready to go to work.

Check for pulse. I couldn't find one.

Check for breathing. Her chest wasn't rising or falling, and I wasn't getting any fogging on the mirror I held in front of her mouth.

"No pulse, no respiration, beginning CPR. You two women, please give us some room.

"I'm the only other person here besides you two ..."

I hadn't really heard what she had said. "We're going to move her to the helicopter. Make sure the two of you don't get in the way. We'll lift on three. One, two, three, lift!"

We moved quickly towards the still open door. I was already going through the list in my head of what we'd do in order to give this woman the best chance to survive. First though I had to make sure the other two were going to be okay until the other units arrived.

"Are you two going to be okay until the other units arrive?"

I already knew she was frustrated by the look she was giving me, but if there was any question, her clipped tone was enough. "I told you, me and her are the only ones here. There is no one else."

I narrowed my eyes at her thinking that this wasn't the time for stupid games. "Look, I saw the other woman here with you when we were landing. Just let me know you're going to be okay until the other units arrive."

She became defiant. "Look, I don't care what you think you saw, but there isn't anyone else here."

I threw my hands up in exasperation. I was wasting time arguing with her and we had a vic what was flat lining behind us. "Fine, whatever. Are {you} going to be okay until the other units arrive?"

Apparently she got the hint that I was done arguing with her. She nodded her accent. "Is she going to be, okay?"

"We'll do the best we can. Now I need you to back away from the craft."

I slid the door shut and immediately felt the ground fall out from under me as the chopper took to the air. Right before I turned to get back to the work of saving the woman's life, I caught sight of the the second woman, who hadn't been there just a second before, standing next to one another. I blinked, just a fraction of a second, and again, the woman was alone.

41 ROADSIDE MARKER

It had been thirty minutes since the last car had passed by me on the stretch of state highway I was watching. Heck, it had been the only vehicle I'd seen in the hour I'd been sitting there. On most nights this was a good place to catch someone going far above the posted limit, but on this night, it seemed particularly deserted.

I tossed the radar gun on the

passenger seat, it makes no sense to even hold it up when I'd see a car coming towards me for nearly a mile. There'd be plenty of warning, so why waste the energy? I didn't necessarily want to pull over someone for speeding, or worse DUI, but it was nights like this that seemed to drag on.

Through my left window I see a flash of light. From this distance the two headlights merged together giving it the appearance of a single large bulb coming towards me. As they came closer, they seemed to separate until finally two distinct beams could be seen.

I picked up the radar gun and took the reading. I clocked them at eight miles over the limit. Not enough for a ticket in my estimation, but a warning for sure. Plus, it gave me a chance to break up the monotony.

As they came closer their headlights illuminated the shoulder of the road. I see a dark figure, unmoving, staring towards the ground. It's too far away for me to make out any details, but it is clearly a person.

The dangers of someone in dark clothing on a state highway at night far outweighs that of a minor traffic violation. The car drives passed me, and I immediately see brake lights as they slow after seeing my patrol car. They're not getting pulled over today, but they don't know that. The taillights aren't nearly as bright, but they do enough to show the silhouette of the cloaked figure, still standing about 100 feet away.

As the car disappears from view so does my dark companion. I turn on my spotlight and swivel it towards where the person was standing. I pass it back and forth along the edge of the road, but I fail to find anything or anyone nearby. I pull out onto the road, hoping to catch whoever had been there a moment ago. The last thing I wanted was to be called back here because of a pedestrian being hit by an oncoming car.

I moved slowly down the road, panning the beam of my spotlight back and forth along the edge and into the brush beyond. Other than the standard weeds and grass I didn't see any sign of the suddenly absent individual.

A shadow moved passed the light. It was too fast for me to make out what it was, but it seemed to be moving back towards where I had first spotted something. I panned my light over, and sure enough, the dark figure stood.

I couldn't see any face, but he was staring down at some point in the grass, seemingly oblivious to the fact that I had my light trained on him. From where I sat, I could see his shoulders seem to shudder slightly as if he was crying. I reached down and flicked on my flashers and pulled towards him.

For the first time this seemed to get a reaction from him as he turned his head towards me. His face was pale white and where his eyes should be there only appeared to be black holes. The effect was startling and had me pressing myself deeper into the seat.

He turned and started walking away along the side of the road. It wasn't until he reached the edge of the light that I snapped out of it. I moved the handle in order to follow him, but he wasn't there. I jerked the light back and forth, up and down, but there was nobody on the road. Somehow, he had simply vanished.

Curious as to what the person had

been looking at, I drove up and parked. I didn't like the idea of exiting my car, fearing the man may reappear, but I had no way of seeing what had caused him such distress without getting out.

I left my door open and the keys in the ignition as I made my way slowly around the edge of the car. Sure, it meant there was a chance someone could take my cruiser, but if the pale-faced man showed up I was going to make a run for it. When I did make it to the other side it didn't take me long to see what was there, a small pink cross had been placed in the dirt.

I'd seen this exact thing many times before. Usually, friends and family placed the memorial to pay tribute to a person who died in an accident at the location. This one being small and pink, I assumed it was a young girl who had been killed here and the man I saw was her father. It was no wonder he was crying.

I made my way back to the car. We didn't have many fatalities in this area, and it wouldn't take much of a search to confirm my suspicions. Within a few minutes I had located the report of a single car wreck that had claimed the lives of two people. I scanned through the text and found that a seven-year-old girl had died in the crash. The next line brought the hair up on the back of my neck, the other victim had been her father.

42   SOS

We were six miles off the coast of Maine, lurching through the swells and troughs as we made our way deeper into the storm. Millions of drops of water slammed against the side of the radio communications shack I was sitting inside of in a seemingly endless torrent of wind and water.

Our Captain had us heading in the direction of an emergency call from a small fishing vessel that had been damaged to do the heavy storm and was quickly taking on large amounts of water. We already knew the ship was going to be a loss, our job was to make sure as many of the six man crew didn't suffer the same fate.

The bow of our ship plunged down the back side of a wave that made it feel as if we were completely vertical only to be lifted back up at an equally leg wrenching angle. Everything that had long since been secured in place, so they weren't flying around the interior. This didn't stop me from hearing everything vibrating in their respected places.

We were moving northeast towards a set of coordinates that had been given to us by the captain of the vessel. When we tried to verify them with Atlantic Command, they told us they had heard no such transmission. It had come in clearly to me, including the name and home birth of from which it came, both of which I had given them and asked for more information on the vessel.

We were coming up on a mile from the coordinates, still almost 10 minutes before we arrived. I radioed the captain, so he would know our location and what direction we would be approaching him from. his response was panicked, more screaming and begging for help than anything that would tell me that he had received my message. I repeated it again, this time asking him to verify that he had received it.

"Mayday, mayday... this is Vessel ... We have lost power and are ... please help!" The broken message did little to verify that he had heard me.

I scanned the surface of the water as we crested a wave looking for some sign of the other ship. Before I could see anything, we dipped down, stealing my view. Trying to give our position I reached over and began using our signal light in an attempt to establish some sort of communication. About this time, we rose up again, giving me a moment to look out over the water.

By this time I was sure we would

have some sort of visual contact if they were still afloat. I tried radioing them again, this time though I didn't get any response, just silence. I feared that we had lost them, but I didn't see any sign that a ship had been here at all.

I was double checking my coordinates that had been given to me when my radio came to life. It was Atlantic Command, not the fishing vessel. They asked me to repeat the name of the ship we had received the communication from and the captain's name. It was an odd request, but I complied with it. Usually, Command gives you some sort of response, but this time nothing came back.

"Do you copy on that information?" I asked after a few seconds.

"Are you sure that is the ship you received the distress call from?" was their response.

At this point in time I was starting to get frustrated with the situation. The other ship still hadn't come into view, and we were right on top of the coordinates where they were supposed to be. Even if they had drifted due to the storm, we would have been able to see them at this point. On top of that I had Atlantic Command asking me to verify information over and over again.

"Yes, I'm sure that is the vessel. Is there a problem?"

A brief pause followed, then finally a response. "From the records we have, that particular ship and everyone aboard was lost at sea."

This seemed obvious, and my response seemed to indicate that. "Yes, they will be if we can't find them. What's your point?"

"No, you don't understand, that ship was lost, six years ago."

I heard the words, but I didn't quite understand what they meant. "Sorry, come back with that last message. Did you say that ship sunk six years ago?"

"Roger, that's what we're saying.

Everything we have on it says that the ship and all six crew were lost."

This conversation went on for a few more minutes as we checked to see if there were any other vessels with the same name, but there were none. The only one was the lost ship. Just to make sure we circled around for a while to see if we could find any sign of the missing ship, but in the end, we turned back to port without finding a soul.

When we got back, I pulled the recordings of the radio traffic, hoping to hear the call we had received. During the times when the traffic came in though, all you could hear was my responses. The radio of the other ship was missing.

43 HOUSE CALL

May 27, 1972

"Do you see that car up there?"

"What car?"

"The one that keeps swerving."

"You think he's drunk? Or just a bad driver?"

"Both?"

They laughed as one of them, Officer Jones of the California Highway Patrol, flipped on the siren of their cruiser. He sped up to pull behind the car. The car began slowing and heading to the side of the road.

Once stopped, the second, Officer Matthews, radioed in the plates of the car.

"That car was just reported stolen," returned the voice on the radio. Jones and Matthews looked to each other, surprised. They got out of the cruiser and began slowly walking towards the car.

Officer Jones went up to the window. It was still rolled up. He knocked on it. The suspect inside rolled it down.

"Hi there," said Jones. "Could you step out of the car for a minute? And keep your hands where I can see them."

"Is something wrong?" asked the suspect, trying to act innocent and doing a terrible job.

"Please step out of the car with your hands up."

Officer Matthews came around and got out his handcuffs.

The suspect stepped out of the car. He was big; nearly 6'6". Body of a football player. The officers were intimidated.

"You're under arrest for driving a stolen vehicle," said Matthews as grabbed the hands of the suspect. He began to tell the suspect his Miranda rights.

He had gotten one wrist into the handcuffs and was attempting to put the other in when the suspect flailed, knocking Matthews back. The suspect's hands were free, and Jones unsheathed his gun, but the suspect managed to swat it out of his hand.

The suspect jumped on Matthews, now on the ground, and they began wrestling. Jones, panicking, went for his gun on the ground a few feet away.

The suspect managed to grab the gun from Matthews. He pointed it at Jones, now reaching for his gun. The suspect fired twice, hitting Jones in the elbow and the stomach.

Jones cried out in pain and collapsed on the ground. Matthews screamed as the suspect got up and pointed the gun at him.

"Please," said Matthews, crying. The suspect fired, hitting him in the knee. Matthews collapsed, screaming in pain. The suspect fired twice more, hitting him in the arm and chest, before running to his car, starting it in a frenzy, and driving off.

Matthews and Jones lay there, unable to move, bleeding out.

***

Long ago, I was playing in my room. I had to go to the bathroom, so I ran down the hall. That was when it happened.

I ran out of the bathroom, a little scared but mostly just annoyed, and ran to my mom's room. She wasn't there. I ran downstairs, looking in the living room and dining room. I finally found her in the kitchen.

"Mommy!" I said urgently.

"What?" she asked. She looked concerned.

"I really have to go potty!"

"Ok, why don't you go?"

"I can't go because there's a man in the bathroom!"

She looked alarmed and immediately got up.

"What?"

"There's a man in there. And I don't want to go in front of him."

"Are you sure?"

"Yes. Mommy, can you make him go away?"

She ran to the garage and came back with a baseball bat. She began walking upstairs, slowly, and I followed her. I remember being annoyed at how slow she was going; I must've really had to go.

She called out, "Hello?"

There was no answer.

She called out, "Is someone there?"

Nothing.

She got upstairs, and walked down the hallway. I was right behind her.

One last time, she called out, "Hello?"

Nothing.

She stepped to the bathroom and slowly opened the door. She evidently didn't see anything. She stepped in, brandishing the baseball bat, and waved it behind the door. She paused before opening the curtain to the shower.

Nothing.

I stepped in, and saw him there. Standing by the toilet.

"There, Mommy!" I said, pointing.

She jumped around, terrified. But she didn't see him.

"What?"

"Do you not see him, Mommy?"

"No sweetie, I don't. What does he look like?"

"He's a police officer," I said quietly.

"A police officer? What color is his uniform?"

"Tan."

"CHP," she said under her breath. "Ok, sweetie, don't worry because he's not real. He can't hurt you."

A tear began rolling down my cheek. "But he looks so scary."

"What do you mean?"

"He's all bloody. He was shooted, and he has holes in his elbow and tummy." She looked at me, bewildered.

I continued. "And the other one -"

"- there's another one?" she interrupted.

"In my room."

We walked to my room. She didn't see him.

"What does this one look like?" she asked.

"He's also a tan police officer. And he has holes in his leg and arm."

I remember a look coming over her face as she heard about these two officers I was seeing. At the time, I had no idea what it meant.

It was only later, much later, that my mom told me what had happened. I was in my twenties, home for Thanksgiving. We were all sitting around for dinner. We talked about all kinds of stuff.

At one point, my brother and I got into our yearly tradition of going through old memories of our childhood. Invariably, the story of the police ghosts came up.

I started telling it, and my mom listened solemnly. It could've been the wine, or the warm atmosphere, but she just quieted right down. She was usually so talkative.

After the meal, she sat down on the couch next to me.

"Did I ever tell you the backstory of those ghosts?"

"Backstory?"

She looked at me with her big blue eyes, and took a moment to compose her thoughts.

"You know how I worked for the Sherriff's department, back before you were born? Well, soon after I left, there was an incident."

She told me about the incident. About Jones and Matthews, and the stolen car.

"Jones was a really close friend of mine," she said quietly. "Around the time that you saw those ghosts, the trial to convict the murderer was getting started. They didn't reveal the names of the two officers who had been killed. But I had a hunch it was Jones. One of my friends still in the department managed to help me out, get me the file. And it confirmed what I thought; Jones was one of the officers who had been killed."

She took a moment to let this sink in. "When you saw those ghosts, I had this strange feeling that one of them was Jones. I almost was sure of it."

"Do you have a picture of him?" I asked, intrigued. Her eyes lit up, and she went off to her room. She returned ten minutes later, holding a picture in her hand. She gave it to me, and I looked at it.

My jaw dropped. I couldn't believe my eyes. There he was. The ghost.

She could tell by the look on my face. A tear began rolling down her cheek, and I hugged her.

"Why do you think he came to our house?" I finally asked.

"I've been wondering that for years. You know, for a while I was in denial that you had seen anything.

That maybe you were just doing a weird joke. Or you were tired, or something. But now I know."

I smiled at her, and gave her another hug.

44 GUNNED DOWN

While I was growing up, my mother worked as a police officer in a city back east. She had her share of stories of crazy things she had seen or experienced during her time as a cop. My mother did her best to try and keep from bringing her work home with her, but there was one time that she did just that and didn't even realize it had happened.

I was only about eight years old when this happened. I was watching television with her when I had the urge to use the restroom. I got up and walked to the bathroom down the hall. The first thing I noticed about him was he wore a police uniform similar to the one my mother had. The second was he had little red patches all over his uniform, including the largest right in the center of his chest. The odd thing was he didn't seem to even notice that they were there. He just stood there staring at me.

It wasn't uncommon for my mother to invite one of her fellow officers over for dinner, but I had met all of them beforehand, and I'd never seen this guy before. Not wanting to be rude, I excused myself from the bathroom, figuring he was trying to clean whatever he had on his shirt off. I went back out to the living room to ask my mom if I could use the bathroom in her bedroom.

"What's wrong with the one down the hallway?" she asked me.

"The other policeman is in there," I

told her.
She gave me a puzzled look for a second. "What do you mean there is a policeman in the bathroom?"

I described to her that the man seemed to be in there trying to clean all the red stains he had gotten on his uniform. As soon as I got done telling her, she took off down the hallway and threw open the bathroom door. Caught off guard by my mother's reaction to just a stain on a shirt, I reached the bathroom a few seconds after she did. I looked around, but there was no sign of the officer anywhere.

"Go out to the living room and wait for me to come get you." My mom's voice left no room for argument.

As I sat down on the couch, I watched as my mom meticulously went from room to room, searching for the officer that I had seen. After she had searched the entire house, she came back to the living room and asked me what the man looked like that I had seen. Now I can appreciate that she didn't doubt I'd seen something. Even from a young age, I wasn't one to make up something like this.

When my mom asked me to describe what the officer looked like, I did my best to recount every detail that I could remember. The things that seemed to stick out the most to me were the red splotches all over his body. My mom did her best to try and keep a calm demeanor, but as my description went on, I could see her posture became rigid.

After I got done speaking, she stood up and went to the phone and called somebody. I couldn't make out what she was saying, but from her tone, I could tell that she wasn't happy with the person she was speaking to. When mom was done with her phone call, she came back and sat next to me. "Are you sure you saw that man in the bathroom?"

"Yeah, Mom, I'm sure. Why, is everything okay?"

"Have you watched the news at all today?" The question caught me off guard. I mean, what kind of 10-year-old watches the news?
"I haven't watched any television. What's going on?"

The energy in her body seemed to drain from her in one big huff of breath. "Honey, something happened today, and I don't want you to worry." As expected, worrying was exactly the thing I started to do. "While I was at work today, a man was shot, a fellow officer."

My young brain had yet to connect the dots. "Is he okay?"

"Sweety, he didn't make it."

I knew that when another officer dies in the line of duty that all of them take it very hard whether they were close or not. They are a family.

"Oh..." was all I could think to say at the time.

"The thing is the man you described in the bathroom and the places that you said he had the red spots all over him..." I nodded my understanding, "... you gave a very good description of him, including where he had been struck by the bullets."

I heard what was said but what she wasn't telling me was that there would have been no way for me to know where the man had been shot. These were details that hadn't been released to the media. Somehow, I had been able to describe in detail the exact location of his injuries.

I don't understand why the spirit of that dead officer was in the bathroom that night. My mom later on told me that she knew the man, but they were not close. I still can vividly recall the injuries I saw on the man, even all these years later. It is a memory I will carry with me for a long time.

45 STROLLER

For as long as I can remember, I had always wanted to work in a field where I could help people. As I got older, I found myself drawn towards the field of EMT. The idea that I could make the difference in someone living or dying just had a certain nobility, and as a person who wanted to serve the greater good, I thought that this was my calling.

Two years into my first job, I was working the night shift. Most nights were pretty busy, but on occasion, you would get the one where you would sit in the bay of the hospital just waiting for a call to come in. In this line of work, boredom is a good thing since that means no one is hurt. Still, it makes the nights pass slowly.

I had gotten to know many of the other crews that I worked with, and we were sitting out front sipping on our nightly energy drink and chatting about some of the things that we had seen over the past couple of weeks. That is when I saw a woman pushing a stroller across the front of the vehicles. She was probably in her mid-30's and very pretty. She stopped and waved at us four guys before continuing on pushing her baby across the parking lot. It was definitely strange for that time of night, but you never know what someone's schedule might be.

Doing the typical guy thing, we all began to argue who she was actually waving at. All of us insisted that we were the object of her attention while adamantly disputing all three of the other's claims. This went on for about five minutes when I figured it would be a good time to use the bathroom.

I got out of the ambulance and walked through the sliding doors. One of the nurses that I knew could still hear the spirited debate that was still going on between my three buddies.

"What's got them so wound up tonight?" she asked me.

"Oh, just too much testosterone, not enough brains." I joked.

"Really? And what caused that?"

"Oh, some lady with a stroller walked by and waved at all of us, which turned into a competition... what?" Her face just seemed to go slack all of a sudden.

"You said a woman, pushing a baby?" The reaction wasn't the one I was expecting. I had anticipated being called any number of names, but her focus being on the woman and the baby surprised me.

"Yeah, she just stopped and waved, then moved on. Why, what's the big deal?"

"What did she look like?" The nurse was uncomfortable with this conversation. There was a point she was trying to get to, but I didn't know what it was.

I went about describing her the best I could. As I continued to rattle off all the details, I could remember I recall her getting very twitchy. Something was bothering her, so I came out and asked her what the big deal was; it was just a woman waving at some paramedics. That wasn't unheard of.

She pulled out her phone and started typing on it. At first, I thought she was just being rude, but when she turned her phone to me, it had a picture on it. It was of a woman smiling. It bore a striking resemblance to the woman that had waved at us just a few minutes ago.

"Is this her? Is she the woman who waved to you?" Her eyes were wide, waiting for me to answer.

I took one closer look at the picture. "Ya, I think that's her. Why, do you know her?"
"Yeah, I know her. She's dead." What do you say when someone tells you that the woman you just saw outside is dead. My response was something like, "Um... what?" She typed something else on her phone and brought up a news article, and handed it back for me to read. It talked about the death of a young mother who was hit by a drunk driver while pushing her young son down

the sidewalk in a stroller. She had reacted quickly and pushed the stroller out of the way but was struck by the car. She was taken to our hospital and died shortly thereafter. Included in the article was a picture of the woman. It was the same photo the nurse had just shown me.

After finishing with the article, I handed her back the phone. "Is this some kind of sick joke or something?"

She told me that there had been a number of people that have talked about seeing this woman pushing a stroller through the parking lot at various times during the day. She never speaks, just smiles and waves then moves on.
I was having trouble accepting what I was being told. She had been right there, not ten feet in front of us. She didn't look like a ghost; she appeared solid as anyone else. But the evidence right in front of me said otherwise. After using the bathroom,

I went out anxious to tell the three others what I had found out about the woman. I know they would have just as hard of a time believing what I'd been told. But at least with three other witnesses, I wouldn't feel like I was going crazy.

When I got out to the truck, the other vehicle was missing. They had received a call and had responded to it while I was in the bathroom. When I told my partner about it, he didn't say anything. He just said I was crazy and wouldn't speak on the subject. I know what I saw, and even though he won't acknowledge it, he knows he saw it too.

46 SHOWING UP

A few summers ago, I was doing some overtime on the overnight shift. I was routed to a neighborhood for a possible breaking and entering. On the way there, the information that we had suggested that a young female had woken up to a man watching her in her bedroom while she slept. We live in a very tight-knit community, so the possibility of a child predator was especially troubling. The name of the people was familiar to me, but I couldn't place where I had seen it before.

When I arrived at the house, all the lights in the residence were on, including the front porch light. I grabbed my clipboard and knocked on the front door. It took only a few seconds, and I saw someone coming towards the door. I announced that I was a police officer, and the person undid the locks.

The woman who answered it was in her late 30's to early 40's, and she had a look of panic in her eyes. As a father myself, I could understand how she must be feeling at that very moment. Someone had broken into her home, the place where her family was supposed to be safe, and threatened her child.

She held back a small dog when I told her I was going to have a look around the outside of the house to make sure that the individual wasn't still there. I circled the house with my flashlight looking for possible signs of forced entry like broken windows or where an entrance had been forced open. There was a back door to the house, and I tried the handle to see if it had been left unlocked, but the handle refused to turn. I knew that it was possible it could have been locked after the fact, which happens quite often.

After doing a complete circuit around the house, I didn't find any evidence that someone had broken in.

When I knocked, she invited me in, and I informed her I wanted to do a sweep inside to make sure the intruder wasn't still somewhere in the house. I asked her if there was anyone else there, and she told me it was just her and her daughter and that no one else lived there.
I went room by room, looking in closets and under beds, anywhere I could think a full-grown man might be hiding. Again, I came up empty. All of the windows were latched, nothing seemed out of place. Most of the time, when someone breaks in, they can't help but leave behind traces, dirt on the windowsill,

footprints, things moved around. That wasn't the case here.

Satisfied I'd looked everywhere, I went to the living room where she and her daughter sat on the sofa. The girl had been the one who had seen the intruder. The first thing that I noticed was she didn't seem scared, which given the situation, was quite odd. Given I was here would indicate that the person who had been seen wasn't supposed to be there. Yet she sat on the couch, a smile on her face, kicking her legs as if nothing out of the ordinary had happened.

When her mom told her that she should tell me what she had seen, I remember clearly what she had said.

"Daddy came and saw me."

Of all the things she could have said, that wasn't what I had expected.

Sure, I had some experience where parents had lost custody of their kids for one reason or another, especially in the field that I work in. Sometimes parents do some strange things when this type of thing occurs.

The reaction of most parents when this happens is fairly typical. They get angry. But this woman didn't. She seemed almost exhausted by the answer like she'd heard it before and was tired of it. She told her daughter that her dad didn't come to see her. That he couldn't, and she knew that. At this point, my first reaction was thinking that he was possibly incarcerated and had been for some time. I was wrong.

She must have felt like she had to explain why he couldn't have come to see his daughter. It turned out that the girl's father was a man that had been killed a couple of years prior in a rollover accident in which he was killed on his way to pick her up from a friend's house. She had waited for hours for him to show up only to find out later what had happened. The whole town had heard the story, and now I knew why the name of the family had been familiar; the story had been widely reported around the area.

The mother apologized to me and told her daughter to tell the truth, that I could be trusted. Even after these reassurances, the little girl insisted that the man she had seen in her bedroom was her father.

I asked her to describe for me what the man looked like. She described a man that was of average height, with curly brown hair and blue eyes. Essentially this guy could have been just about anyone, but then she mentioned he had a small scar on the right side of his upper lip. This at least gave me something to work with.

She seemed uncomfortable as if she

wanted to say something else but wasn't sure whether she should. I decided to just wait her out and see if she would talk on her own. When she didn't continue, I decided to push just a little. "Was there something else you remember about him?"

She just looked down at her hands which she was fiddling with in her lap and nodded. When she didn't speak, her mom urged her to continue. "It's okay; you can tell us." It was obvious that she hadn't heard this part either. "He was clear."

At first, I thought she meant she had clearly seen him. "You mean you saw him clearly."
"No, like he was see-through."

At the mention of this detail, her mother got upset and told her it wasn't okay to lie, especially to the police. I could see that she was starting to doubt whether her daughter had actually seen something or she had made up the entire story. I understood her reaction. To me, it sounded like this girl was telling us she had seen a ghost.

It seemed most likely at this point the girl might have been dreaming and had mistaken the dream for something real. These types of calls happen where a person swears they saw someone, but it turns out to be nothing. Still, I didn't want to leave without making sure.
"Are you sure you weren't just having a dream?"

"No, he was there. We talked to each other. I swear!" It felt like she was defending what she had said like she had to convince us that she hadn't lied about the entire thing. "Mom, he told me to tell you, 'I love you, peanut.' What does that mean?"

At the word 'peanut,' her mother

flinched as if she'd been struck.
"What did you say?"
Something about the phrase had hit home. "He said, 'I love you peanut.'"

"Ma'am, does that mean something to you?"
She stared at the wall in front of her for a moment, then turned towards me. "Peanut, he used to call me that before she was born. I hated it, so he stopped."

"Has she ever heard him call you that before?" I gestured to her daughter.
She shook her head. "No, this was back before she was born."

The conversation had taken a lot of turns in a short period of time. Somehow this had gone from a breaking and entering to a child's dream, and now something else.

We all just sat there waiting for

someone to speak. It was her mother that broke the silence. "Officer, I'm sorry for wasting your time."

I was clearly being dismissed, and given the direction, this was headed, I was fine with leaving. "I'll file a report. If something else comes up, please don't hesitate to call."
She shut the door after me with a simple: "Thank you for your help, officer."

That call has stuck with me since it happened. I'm not entirely sure what to believe. Is it possible that the spirit of the girl's father had visited her? It seemed that both of them thought so. Maybe it was the dad showing up for his daughter, to give her a chance to say goodbye, to get some closure.

47 INSIDE THE CELLBLOCK

It had only been a few weeks since I had gotten my transfer from the Chicago police department to a smaller, quieter location. After years of discussions, my wife had finally convinced me that it would be better, and safer, if I was working in a place where there wasn't so much violent crime. The dangers of my job, and the stresses that came with it, was taking its toll on our marriage. In the end, a decision had to be made, I applied at a few local precincts, and after a couple months I started working as a jailer.

One of the hardest parts of transferring into a new job is you end up getting one of the less desirable shifts. Right off the gate, I was posted on the overnight crew. I still hadn't gotten used to the late-night hours, especially since most days the place was empty except for the occasional drunk that was pulled off the road.

Most nights I passed the time roaming the two small cellblocks in an attempt to fight off the inevitable drowsiness. This night was no different. I looked over at the clock, 1:24 am, nearly five and a half hours left before I got to go home and get some sleep. There hadn't been a call all night, meaning neither of the other two units had come in to do some paperwork and offer a little company.

Out of nowhere I thought I heard a light rattling noise. The sound was very soft and had ended quickly, enough to have me questioning whether I had heard anything at all. For a moment I held still, even my breath paused in my lungs as I listened for it again.

Seconds passed, yet the air remained devoid of any sound. I had nearly convinced myself that it was just my imagination when it happened again, louder this time.

The noise was coming from one of the cell blocks, but there wasn't anyone housed there. Just the past hour I walked the floor and looked in every cell. Nobody was in them.

I'd heard noises like this before. Drunks would come to and grab the handles to the closed cells and shake them in an attempt to get out only to find they had been locked in. With an empty cellblock though I considered other possibilities water pipes, heating vents, maybe an animal had gotten trapped somewhere... The most likely option was an animal somewhere, since the first two options hadn't happened in the time I had been working there.

I sighed and grabbed my flashlight so I could go and take a look. The rattling noise had become so loud at this point, sounding as if someone was violently shaking the door. My confidence that it was an animal was quickly beginning to fade. My hands shook as I held the key in front of the lock, my courage draining by the second.

I really don't want to go in there... I was a seasoned vet in a city where I took my life into my hands every day, yet I hadn't been more afraid in my life.

The first time I tried to put the key in I missed the hole by almost an inch. Somehow, I manage it on the second try. I turn the key, disengaging the lock. Somehow, as if I have flicked a switch, the rattling comes to a sudden stop.

My mind screams for me to get away, but my body seems frozen in place, my muscles betraying me. I stay that way for almost a minute before I can move again. Much as I want to shut the door, I know I have to go inside.

I push the door revealing the six cells that line the wall to the right. I can't see anyone from outside the door, but my gut tells me that something is *there.*

"Hello?" I call.

Nothing answers me back, but the

hairs on the back of my neck stand on end. In my gut I *know* someone, or something is watching me, waiting for a moment of weakness. My eyes automatically find the corners of the room, seeking out a possible source of the discomfort, only to come up empty.

No one is in here, stop acting like a child. What would the other officers say if they saw you like this?

I don't have to answer that question. The shame pushes me into the room. No hidden figure jumps out at me, but the temperature drops significantly, enough that I can now see my breath come out of my mouth in little puffs.

I move quickly, looking in one door after another. The further I go into the tier, the colder it seems to get. By the time I reach the last door, I'm shivering. I briefly turn to look inside and catch a dark form sitting on the bed. I step back to look again, surprised by what the unexpected turn only to find the bed empty.

Standing there, shivering and confused, I feel something touch the back of my neck. The suddenness of it shocks me enough that I make a mad rush for the door. I sprint through, and slam it shut behind me.

By the time I'm able to have a coherent thought, I'm standing at my post, doubled over with my hands on my knees. My mind races, trying to make sense of what has just happened. A loud bang came from behind the door and then quite descended over the jail once more, this time for good.

48 WEEPING JESUS

I've seen a lot of strange things during my ten years as a firefighter. Even in a small town like mine, this job brings you face to face with some of the stranger aspects of life. A forest fire that began with a little kid trying to kill ants with a magnifying glass, refracting the light until the dry brush ignited. A blaze set to cover up the scene of a gruesome crime. I've even gotten a couple of calls for the cliche cat stuck in a tree situation. The strangest thing by far, however, happened when I was still just a rookie.

About seven or eight years ago, we arrived at a townhouse with heavy fire from the first floor on side one. Someone had fallen asleep with a frozen pizza in the toaster oven. Luckily, the residents managed to make it out before it was too late, and as they received oxygen from the EMT's we set about putting out the flames.

After making entry, locating the fire in the kitchen, and extinguishing it, we set about taking out a few windows for ventilation. After the smoke had risen, we noticed that the living area to the rear of the kitchen (which was on the right-hand side as we entered) had taken significant smoke and heat damage. All of the furniture was badly singed, if not completely reduced to ash. The walls were streaked black with smoke. The only thing that looked unharmed by the fire was a framed image, hanging above the mantle. On the wall was a picture of Jesus Christ, the only object in the room that appeared untouched. It defied the laws of smoke and fire, and the strangest thing of all is that even the wall BEHIND the picture was smoke-stained and blistered. For lack of a better word, it seemed miraculous. But that wasn't all… There was evidence of two streams of water that had trickled from the painting to a point in the middle of the wall where they met and continued down to the floor. Upon closer examination, it looked almost as if the image of Christ was weeping, the bubbled marks of water the only damage on the canvas, streaming forth from the eyes of the Holy man. My friend, another rookie firefighter, was the first to notice. He muttered something in Spanish and crossed himself, sending up a prayer of thanks. Being more logical than spiritual, I sought an explanation. Perhaps spray from the hose or even steam.

The odd thing was that the line had been pulled through this room and was flowing into the kitchen to push the fire out the front, through a large, vented window. No water had been moving through the room, and the steam produced had been pushed out the window. Still, I was skeptical. I was curious to hear what the Fire Marshall would say. However, to my surprise, even he was amazed.

"The greatest anomaly of my career," is what he called it.

The woman who owned the townhouse was a devout Christian. When we told her about the painting she fell to her knees, weeping. She said Christ saved her life. It was difficult to argue with.

Later, the local paper wrote about the fire. When they interviewed the homeowner, she told them about the painting, and how she believed her faith saved her that day. The journalist confirmed with the Fire

Marshall and the story became a piece of local lore. Everyone in our sleepy little town knew about weeping Jesus, as he came to be known. The Catholic church nearby even claimed it as a miracle, and worshipers from neighboring cities would travel to see the burned-up townhouse.

The woman who owned the house, and the painting, kept it above her bed until her dying day. She passed away recently of old age. Her memorial was attended by many community members, and I felt compelled to pay my respects. I learned not too long after that the woman had a plan for the painting after her passing. She gave it to the local fire department.

Now, the unblemished image of weeping Jesus hangs in a prominent place in our little firehouse, serving as both a lucky charm and a reminder that miracles are possible. While I am not a woman of faith, I can't help but look up at the image's softly smiling face and wonder… Did Christ really save a life that day?

49 RUN AWAY

When I was a municipal cop, I was sent to a missing person runaway juvenile call. The town I worked in was inner city and poor, and it wasn't uncommon for children to go missing or run off, unfortunately. Even more horribly, it wasn't unheard of that parents would make their children… disappear, in some way or another. It was a tough place to work and because of that, I was rarely fazed. Except for this one night.

This call was a little different than usual because it was one of the better streets in town, and the family was squared away. The husband and wife were both educators and known in their church and community to be loving and generous. They had two daughters, the older of which was the one who had gone missing. When I arrived the family was in shambles, understandably. The mother had woken up in the middle of the night and decided to check on the girls. When she opened the door to the older daughter's room she was greeted by an open window and an empty bed.

I asked the parents if they thought their daughter might have run away. It didn't seem likely to me, given the circumstances, so I was surprised when the couple exchanged a shifty glance. I narrowed my eyes and pushed a little harder. What was it? Did she have a boyfriend they didn't approve of? Was she showing signs of mental stress? Had she ever talked about going somewhere else? To every question, the partners answered no, but I could tell they were holding something back.

"Did she seem unhappy or discontented in any way?" I asked, getting frustrated. They again exchanged a strange look. I reminded them gruffly that I couldn't help them unless they helped me. The mother began to sob.

"You're going to think we're crazy," she said. I felt my stomach twist. Before I could figure out what she meant by that, however, the younger tottered into the room, a teddy bear still clasped in her little hand.

"Daddy," she said, "I see grandma in the hall."

With that, she pointed down the long, unlit hallways off the living room where we were seated. I looked in the direction she was gesturing but saw nothing. When I looked back at the parents they were as white as sheets. The father leapt to his feet and raced down the hall, turning on every light he could find as he did so. His behavior was strange, and I started to feel more and more uneasy.

When he returned a few moments later he looked ill. He took his seat and looked up at me with wild eyes. "Officer, did you see her? Did you see my mother?"

I told him I had not, and asked him why it was remarkable that his mother had walked down the hallway. The husband pressed his palms against his face and shook his head before he replied. "She died last year," he finally admitted. "And I know how this sounds, I really do, but…we see her walking around the house all the time." I gulped. That was a first.

"If our daughter ran away, that's why," the wife said through her tears.

"She saw his mother, the thing, first. It terrifies her. She says she can't sleep at night. She says she doesn't want to live in a haunted house."

Their story was strange, to say the least. At the time I was unconvinced by anything they said. I requested they come down to the station to answer a couple more questions. They hesitantly agreed, and as I led the couple and their second child down the driveway to my cruiser, I turned and looked back at the house one last time. What I saw made me feel sick.

For just a fleeting moment, I swear I saw an old woman standing in the upstairs window, her bony frame backlit by the lights that the father left on. Then, I blinked, and she was gone. I tried to brush it off, remain professional, and keep my cool. Someone noticed, however. It was the little girl. She looked up at me with big blue eyes and asked, "Did you see grandma too?"

It still gives me goosebumps to think about that house and that night. It turns out that the teenage daughter had snuck out because she couldn't sleep. She'd been doing it for weeks, just taking walks around the park before coming home at daylight. Her parents were relieved beyond measure, and I warned her not to do something so dangerous ever again. She agreed, and as she walked away from the station with her family, back to that terrifying place, I couldn't blame the girl for wanting to run away. I too had seen the face of the old woman in the window. I didn't sleep for a week.

50 NIGHT AT THE CASINO

I was working as an EMT and security officer at a casino. I was the newbie. There was always a bit of playful hazing among the staff when somebody joined the team, and as someone who perhaps takes myself a little too seriously at times, it wasn't my favorite part of the job. The other security officers would often send me to deal with the drunkest and most belligerent customers, or tell scary stories about ghosts that roamed the halls when no one else was around. I tried to brush it off and do my job. I was there for a paycheck, after all, not to make friends.

One day, about two weeks into the gig, I was walking the parking structure around 0300 hours. Up the hill, by the top-level of the garage, were some street lights, a guard rail, and a road leading up to a water tower, but nothing else. As I made my rounds, I noticed that night seemed especially dark somehow, the street lights dimmer than usual. Still, through the dark, I caught sight of a figure.

It was tough to make out, appearing to be dressed in all black, almost like a walking shadow. I felt a shiver travel down my spine. Usually, nothing scares me. I'm a big guy and almost always armed with a weapon of some kind. If anything, I should be the one people are afraid to encounter on a dark evening. Still, something about the figure just felt... off. I couldn't tell if it was looking down the hill at me or up the hill towards the tower, their face obscured. In either case, the figure was still as stone, just staring off in one direction.

"Hey!" I called out, trying my best to sound threatening. I was shocked to hear that my voice was shaking. What had come over me, I wondered. The figure didn't respond. No turn, no movement, no reply. Only stillness and silence. My heart began to beat faster I didn't have a

flashlight on me so I decided to go grab one before investigating. Keeping my eyes on the figure the entire time, I went down one level and met up with another officer and told him about what I'd seen, secretly hoping he'd come with me to confront them "Aw, you need a nightlight, big boy?" he teased.
I seethed but took the flashlight anyway, determined to figure out what the hell was going on. It'd been some time now and the silhouette was still immobile, my gaze trained on the hill where they stood. The other officer made another snarky comment as I started off with the flashlight and with a flash of anger I turned around to snap back.
"Fuck off and do your job," I
told him. He got quiet after that.

When I turned back around, however, the figure was gone. Not only that, but the dim lights seemed to have returned to normal, the moon once again illuminating the previously pitch-black hill. I turned around, wanting to ask the other officer if he had seen it too. His expression answered for me. Our momentary squabble forgotten, we stared at each other in matching shock.

That officer and I did end up becoming friends eventually, against all odds. Perhaps that night had something to do with it. I found out later that there had been a number of sightings in the area and on levels 5-7 of the garage. It wasn't all hazing, there really was something strange happening at that place. Both of us had a handful of other unexplainable encounters throughout our time there, until the building eventually burned down in a massive fire. Apparently, when the casino was put in they had to move an old Indian cemetery and the sightings started soon after that. It was believed by many in the nearby town that it had been cursed because of that. Believe what you will about the casino and the burial ground but I know one thing for certain. That was no prank I witnessed, but something much darker. Something that made me afraid.

SNEAK PEAK

The Haunting of Emily Blake

Coming 2021-2022

1

ARRIVAL

The SUV eased around the corner through a gap in the trees barely wide enough for it to fit through. It had taken them almost twenty minutes to find this road if you could call it that. Out here it was hard to tell the difference between a path and just a place where a tree wasn't growing. Finally, Emily had found a small cut through the thick trunks and had been crawling along what she hoped was the driveway for the past ten minutes. A little unsure of her decision, Emily nursed her bottom lip with light nibbles. If she had been mistaken it was going to be near impossible to turn around without hitting something.

Emily leaned forward nearly pressing herself against the steering wheel. "I think it's starting to thin out."

This being the third time she'd said the same exact words and only uncomfortable silence greeted her. Joy, who usually was the loquacious one, remained silent. This time however, the words proved to be accurate. They emerged from the trees into a meadow covered in wild grasses. They bent and swayed in the wind making it seem as if the ground itself was golden body of water.

"See, I told you it was clearing up." Emily said.

James leaned forward between the gap in the front seats. "You were bound to be right eventually, Em."

Emily narrowed her eyes at him in mock anger. "With that attitude I should have left you behind."

"You wouldn't have left me. Besides, you two would be bored by yourselves with only each other to talk to."

Joy looked up from her laptop. "So, I've been trying to find some information on this place... what?"

James fell back into his seat in the rear of the car laughing. "See what I mean? My sis, always the life of the party."

Joy spun back to face him. "What? You mean I'm boring? Just because I want to know..."

"Dear lord." At the sound of Emily's voice, they both crossed their arms and veered out their separate windows.

They stopped on the crest of a small rise giving them a panoramic view of house and the grounds surrounding it. It stood two stories tall with two windows jutting out of the front of its second story. Even in the midday light the windows were dim making the structure look pale in comparison.

Vines and weeds had fled their boundaries and intermixed with grass that had intruded from the field overtaking what had once been the front of the home. Most of the vegetation appeared to be in the throes of death, starved of life-giving nutrients upon a spoiled tract of land.

The paint that at one time had coated the outside had flaked away, scored from the walls by wind driven dust and rain. The corrugated roof was more rust than anything that resembled metal leaving questions as to what protection it offered. If this place had been welcoming to visitors those days were in the past. Now it served as a stark reminder of the irrevocable pursuit of nature to reclaim and return the land to what once was.

"We're staying there?" James tapped lightly on the glass. This was far from the country getaway that he had expected when Emily and his sister offered to let him come with them. "Where did you two find this place?"

Lost in the moment Emily appeared not to hear what he had said. "It's perfect."

James however heard her perfectly and stuck his head between the seats once more. "Um, what? This place is a complete dump, it doesn't even seem like it has power. Joy, how do you plan on using your laptop?"

"The place has a generator out back, at least that's what the information I could find out about it before we rented it said." Joy told him.

James looked back and forth between them and collapsed back into his seat. "You two have lost it. Completely mental."

The road leading to the house became increasingly rough and the truck bounced and vibrated as the tires rolled over the washboards and pits that littered the surface. They rounded one final corner and pulled to a stop. The building seemed to loom above them in silent challenge. The deterioration on the outside was even more apparent from this distance as even the smaller blemishes became visible. Up close the house drew them in, it was as if the harder they tried to gaze away the more they had to stare it.

"Well, how about we go check out the inside?" Emily asked them both as she pulled the keys from the ignition.

James craned his neck to see the building out the front of the truck windshield. "Or we could go back and find a hotel to stay in."

Joy rolled her eyes and shut her laptop. "Oh, I'm sure glad we brought along a big strong man to keep us womenfolk safe." she said in her best southern accent.

Emily laughed at the offended look James gave his sister. "Come on James, where's your sense of adventure?"

With that Emily opened her door and got out of the SUV. She stretched trying to ease the stiffness of driving from her limbs. "I mean look at this place. It's freaking awesome!"

James looked down the length of the building unconvinced of really what to think. "What kind of person would want to live in a place like this?"

Joy walked by her brother and patted him gently on the back.

"Obviously, someone rugged and tough, something that you know nothing about."

"Hey what's that supposed to mean?"

Joy glanced over her shoulder at her older sibling with her lip stuck out in an exaggerated pout. "Oh, did I offend your delicate sensibilities?"

"Are you going to just stand there or are we going to check this place out?" Emily began picking her way through the dense ground cover towards the front door. Halfway there she spun around and beckoned them to join her. "Come on you two."

Joy captured the front of her brother's shirt and dragged him forward, he didn't fight her, but a look of reservation clouded his face.

Emily and Joy climbed the two wood steps leading to the small landing where the front door stood. Joy reached into her pocket and produced a key. Surprisingly, it is modern rather than something that would more suit a home of its age.

Sliding the key into the cylinder Emily paused and looked back at her two friends. "Are we ready?"

The key turned smoothly in the lock and the door swung open silently on its hinges revealing the first few feet of a darkened room. Emily was the first to pass the threshold into the house followed by Joy. The room was dim, but the windows let in enough light to for them to see the general layout. Dust floated about the place on unseen currents, the tiny bits of the past that had lain dormant upon every surface and in every corner until life was present once more. Emily thought of it as the house finally drawing in a long-awaited breath now that the door was finally open.

A set of wooden plank stairs rose in the center of the room leading to the upper floor of the building. To their right was a primitive kitchen complete with a woodfire stove against one wall. A few cupboards had been hung above the counter for storage. Near one of the windows where a family could look out while enjoying their meal a small round table stood with four chairs.

To the left was a room that probably once was a living room. A few chairs had been arranged haphazardly around the room. They were all straight-back and made of wood, more for utility than comfort. A large worn rug, the original color long since faded covered the center of the floor. On the wall hung a large cross about two feet tall and half as much wide between two oval frames that contained yellowing portraits of an elderly man and woman that appeared to be staring at each other.

James stepped into the room next to Emily and took in the scene. "I'm going to have to find out who their decorator is."

Emily elbowed him in the ribs for the sarcastic remark. "Just go start bringing in our stuff."

He shook his head and strode back out the door leaving Emily and Joy standing just inside the doorway by themselves.

"So how about you check out the rooms upstairs and I see what else is down here?" Joy asked Emily.

"That works, when you see James can you have him drop my stuff upstairs so I can get set up?" Emily responded still admiring the interior.

"Yup, when I see him, I'll send him up." Joy waved and took off down the hallway.

EMILY 2

With every step up the stairs the wood had let out an audible creaking noise. Emily ran her hand along the railing feeling the surface of the wood that had been worn smooth from age. As she climbed higher, the walls closed in around her the amplifying the noise making it appear louder than before.

After a few more steps up, a hallway came into view. It was darker up here and she could only see a solitary door on either side of the passage. The upper floor was silent, Emily couldn't even hear Joy moving around the level below her. Behind her one of the stairs let out a creak as if someone had put their weight on it. She turned around to glance down the stairs only to see them vacant. *Just the house settling. It's old and we're bound to hear a noise or two during the time we're here.*

The air up here was heavier and carried with it the scent of aged wood almost like she was standing in the loft of an ancient barn. There hadn't been a lot of open floor on the landing making the space feel cramped even with just her standing there. So far everything about this house seemed to be designed for a person to be uncomfortable.

With only ambient light to see by, Emily strained to see through the dense shadows that enveloped the rest of the hall. With this in mind she decided to begin with the door closest to her. She moved up to the door on the right side of the hall and tried its handle. Like the front door, it moved without resistance and the door slid open.

Emily tentatively eased into the dark space edging towards the dim outline of light that seeped around the edges of the window. She probed the area in front of her with a hand swinging it back and forth as she cautiously moved further into the bedroom. As she reached the window Emily took hold of the curtains and drew them open. The windows were coated with dust, but enough light was let in to reveal the contents of the room. The room was small and except for an old wooden bedframe that appeared to be only large enough for a child the room is empty. Her gaze scanned the room and she noticed even the walls bared no adornments. There wasn't even a dresser or a closet to store clothes. *It is more like a wooden cell than a bedroom,* Emily thought to herself with a slight shudder.

Leaving, Emily left the shades drawn and the door open to bring allow her to see better. Across the hall she found a similar room lacking any personal touches and even the most basic of furniture.

From down the hall she heard the sound of the stairs squeaking and something smacking into one of the walls followed by a loud thud on the floor of the landing. Curious as to what it was, she glanced around the door frame hesitantly only to see two suitcases on the ground and the back of James' head descending the stairs.

Emily cupped her hand to her mouth to call after him. "Thank you!"

She watched him raise his hand in acknowledgement before bobbing out of view. *Well, now I've just got to find a place to put them.*

Undeterred by the two rooms Emily began going door to door looking for a suitable place to call her own for the foreseeable future. With every failure her optimism waned a little further. She'd already checked eight rooms and none of them had anything but the bedframe in them. With only four more rooms to go it appeared like she would have to just make the best of one of the spartan rooms she'd already seen.

She opened the next door expecting to see much of the same.

The room itself contained the same small bedframe as every other room but her attention was immediately deterred by something else, an aged desk sitting against the next to the window. This was what she had been looking for, truly it was the whole reason she'd come here in the first place. She'd needed a place to write and this home was to be her inspiration, a way to break through the dam that had been constructed in her mind, a way to silence the doubters.

When Emily first understood that she wanted to be a writer the seed of an idea was something that she barely had to nurture. Even the smallest ideas would take on a life of their own and flourish. It had been like a bottomless well that she could dip into any time she wanted. There had been so many ideas it would have been impossible for her to write them all.

This led to her publishing her first book *Without Sleep.* Only months after that her follow up book

If You Tell hit shelves and within months became a *New York Times* Best Seller. She was considered one of the up-and-coming horror writers. Critics and fans alike praised her works and were anxious to see what she would come up with next.

For the past three years her mind had been a breeding ground for cobwebs and dead-end ideas. It wasn't as if the well had gone dry, it was worse than that. Emily seemed to have lost the well entirely. That part of her mind seemed shut off to her now and the pressure of a new release were mounting.

Sure, the Insta-followers with their constant questions of *"When's the next one coming out?"* or *"Are you going to write another one?"* seemed to build in quantity and frequency on a daily basis. Emily had found it somewhat simple to ignore the mounting questions as well as the weekly calls from her publisher as well. Those had all become easy to ignore. However, the comments that referred to her as a "passing fancy" or a "two-hit wonder" those she took personally. These criticisms shook her to her core, scolding her talent like smoldering blades. Emily wanted to prove to herself that she hadn't just gotten lucky with her first two books, that she could actually do this as a career.

She'd tried everything she could think of, even going to a shrink but nothing seemed to help. Emily was about to give up when her friend Joy had suggested that she try getting away, somewhere that she could just focus on the written word. Emily hadn't been completely convinced this would work, after all Joy, a fellow author and best friend, wrote about historic locations. Joy could go pretty much anywhere and find a story, whereas Emily relied on her imagination.

Without any better ideas though, Emily had agreed and had jumped in with both feet. Sure, this place was abandoned, run down, and more than a little creepy but that is the exact type of place that Emily wrote about. She needed this opportunity for inspiration almost as much as she needed air to breathe. It was an opportunity to immerse herself in a building right out of the pages of the story she wanted to write. So, she was determined to make the best of the prospect because if not she didn't know what she would do after this. Writing had always been Plan A, B and C. Not writing would be like losing her hands, she'd be incomplete.

      Almost like she was in a trance Emily walked across the floor to the desk. It was a dark red, if the light hadn't been on it the color would have looked black. The surface although smooth was not a perfect rectangle. The front and back edges waved like someone had left the natural shape of the tree. The legs were simple and without ornamentation, but they didn't detract from the overall beauty of the desk. It was an extraordinary example of craftsmanship.

Emily sat down in the chair and rubbed the top surface. The surface was impossibly smooth almost as if it were made of glass rather than wood. There was history here. She could feel it, memories had been infused into the very materials that surrounded her. What dreams did the people have when they stared through this very window out into the world beyond it? Emily closed her eyes and tried to see back into to the past.

An idea stirred in the back of her mind; it was barely a whisper, but it was there. It took her so much by surprise she let out a little gasp. It felt like seeing an old friend after a long absence. *I need my paper and pen. I have to get started before it's gone.*

Emily got up and half-jogged down the hallway to where James had left her suitcases. Grabbing the handles, she rolled them back to the bedroom bouncing along the floor in her haste. The larger of the two bags held her clothes, it was the smaller one of the two that she cared about at this very moment. She heaved it up on the bedframe and fumbled at the zipper, adrenaline making her hands clumsy.

Finally, she was able to grab hold of the tab and jerked it sideways. The zipper snagged on a piece of fabric as it tried to turn the corner bringing it to an abrupt halt. Emily yanked the piece of metal attempting to force it past the obstruction, but it seemed to only make it worse.

"Come on you piece of junk!" she yelled losing her patience, slapping at the bag in nearly resigned frustration.

Closing her eyes, she took a deep breath in through her nose and out through her mouth trying to calm herself. A little steadier now she backed the zipper up allowing it to move freely once more. Slowly this time she undid the top flap on the suitcase revealing several journals in which she wrote all of her stories and a worn silver pen, the same pen she had written her first two novels with. It was her good luck charm, even if it had failed her recently.

To her surprise the slight hiccup with opening the suitcase hadn't allowed the idea to dissipate in her mind. In fact, it has grown more solid, expanded even in plot and characters. Emily lifted out one of the identical books from the stack but held her hand in place in a moment of hesitation before taking her pen. Fear and doubt bubbled up from her belly and burnt into her chest. She softly shuddered as if shedding the layer of self-doubt, *I can do this. I know it*.

Emily drew the pen from the sleeve that held it in place feeling the familiar weight of it. She knew it was time to find out if she was a writer or an author. To her a writer simply put ink on paper, an author had an intimate relationship with the words she used. The pen wasn't the tool authors used to create with, the words were the instrument. When used correctly they could paint pictures no human eye had ever seen before. They created worlds that people would beg and plead to get lost in.

Emily sat at the desk pen in hand ready to begin. Against the dark wood of the desk the paper looked impossibly white, almost as if it were glowing. The prospect of filling a single page seemed daunting yet alone hundreds of them.

As soon as the pen touched the paper Emily was startled by James' voice. "Hey Emily!" She scrawled a jagged line down the center of the first page before the pen clatters to the floor between her feet. "Just wanted you to know that all our stuff is inside. Joy and I are going to get our rooms set up."

When Emily turned and seared a look at him, James held up both hands in defense and took a couple steps back. "Uh, sorry about that. I just wanted to..."

Emily stood and walked to him a tight smile upon her face. Reaching up she placed her finger on his forehead pushing him out the door. "Out." The word came out like a breath.

Closing the door, she returned to the desk and looked at the zigzagging line across the first page. She scowled in annoyance, *not a good way to start a book.*

Emily bent down to find her pen that had dropped when James had snuck up on her. She ran her eyes across the surface of the floor searching for the misplaced writing instrument but could not find it anywhere. "Where did you go?" As if talking to the inanimate object would make it somehow appear.

Emily crawled under the desk thinking she must have kicked it when she stood up. Emily froze in place as a metallic clink came from right above her head. Cautiously, she scootched back and rose up on her knees so she could see atop the desk. Sitting next to the open journal sat her missing pen.

Please remember to leave a review after reading.

Follow Eve S. Evans on instagram: @eves.evansauthor

or

@foreverhauntedpodcast

Check out our Bone-Chilling Tales to keep you awake segment on youtube for more creepy, narriated and animated haunted stories by Eve S Evans.

Let me know on Instagram that you wrote a review and I'll send you a free copy of one of my other books!

Check out Eve on a weekly basis on one of her many podcasting ventures. Forever Haunted, The Ghosts That Haunt Me with Eve Evans, Bone Chilling Tales To Keep You Awake or A Truly Haunted Podcast. (On all podcasting networks.)

If you love to review books and would like a chance to snatch up one of Eve's ARCs before publication, follow her facebook page:

Eve S. Evans Author

For exclusive deals, ARCs, and giveaways!

ABOUT THE AUTHOR

From the time I was first published to current, (2021) I've learned so much about life and my journey into the paranormal.

I started this journey a few years ago after living in multiple haunted houses. However, it was one house in particular that chewed me up and spit me out you could say.

After residing in that house I wanted answers… needed them. So I began my journey of interviewing multiple people who too have been haunted. Any occuptaion, you name it, I've interviewed them.

What did I learn from my journey so far? I'm honestly not sure if I will ever get the answers I truly desire in this lifetime. However, I am determined not to stop anytime soon. I will keep plugging along, interviewing and ghost hunting. I am determined to find as many answers as I can in this lifetime before it too is my turn to be nothing but a ghost.

I have several books coming out this year and I am very well known for my "real ghost story anthologies", however, these will be mostly fictional haunted house books as I wanted to give myself a new challenge.

If you'd like to read one of my anthologies my reccomedation to start would be: True Ghost Stories of First Responders. In this book I interview police, firemen, 911 dispatchers and more. They share with me some of their creepiest calls that could possibly even be deemed "ghostly."

Also this year I am hoping to get my paranormal memoir out. I want to share my story and journey with everyone. Until then, just know that if you are terrified in your home or thinking you are going crazy with unexplained occurances, you ARE NOT alone. I thought I was going crazy too. But I wasn't.

If you'd like someone to talk to about what is going on in your home but don't know who to turn to, feel free to message me on Instagram or on Facebook.

Forever Haunted Podcast

The Ghosts That Haunt Me with Eve Evans Podcast

A Truly Haunted Podcast

Follow Eve S. Evans on instagram @eves.evansauthor

CPSIA information can be obtained
at www.ICGtesting.com
Printed in the USA
LVHW102248151022
730802LV00003B/92